1

Cloudscapes over the Lune

Short Stories and Poems from Our Valley

By

Clare Weze Easterby

Mary Sylvia Winter

Melissa Bailey

Sarah Dobbs

& Kay Douglas

MAKE·(A·WISH)®

£1.00 from the sale of this book will be donated to
Make-A-Wish Foundation® UK

Make-A-Wish is a charity registered in England and Wales
(295672) and Scotland (SC037479)

Make-A-Wish Foundation® UK has a very simple objective – to
grant magical wishes to children and young people fighting life-
threatening illnesses. The charity was founded in the UK in 1986
and since then has granted over 6,000 wishes.

With over 20,000 children in the UK living with life-threatening
conditions at any one time, our work is never ending. Our aim is
to ensure that every one of these children is able to experience the
magic and joy of a Make-A-Wish wish.

We receive no government funding or lottery grants, relying on
the generous donations of the public and that's why, for our
charity, every donation really counts.

£1.00 from the sale of this book will be donated to Rainbow Trust, Registered Charity No. 1070532.

Rainbow Trust Children's Charity provides emotional and practical support to families who have a child with a life-threatening or terminal illness. Rainbow Trust's Family Support Workers join the family in their own home and are there to provide practical support. We are contactable 24 hours a day for families in crisis from diagnosis, through treatment and even after bereavement.

Rainbow relies almost entirely on voluntary donations and through the generosity of our supporters we are able to help around 1,000 families a year.

For Peter and Dominic

Acknowledgements

Edited by Harvey Stanbrough at StoneThread.com.
Editing and developmental contributions by Bonnie French.
Proofreading and moral support unfailingly provided by Lucy
Nankivell (lucy-n@tiscali.co.uk) and Judith Shaw
(info@judithshaw.co.uk).
Title photographs kindly donated by Helen Lapping, Mike Bone,
Peter Easterby and Gareth Pritchard.
With thanks to Graham Mort and Jo Baker for helping with the
search for contributors, Keith Reeves for inspirational teaching,
Andrew Easterby for supplying farming information and putting
up with the midnight hours and to Annette and Vernon
Waterhouse, for everything.

Contents

Occupied Territory

Clare Weze Easterby

It wasn't the kind of spat that anyone could have predicted. Lori, my daughter-in-law, can be as calm as a boat on a millpond but then, just like the weather, sudden squalls will spurt out of her and all I can do is run for shelter. I'm not a confrontational mother-in-law.

'I can see the ant people,' said little Ben. He had climbed into the seat nearest the kitchen window and was tracing tiny pathways on the glass with his finger.

Lori stopped clearing the children's breakfast bowls and looked across at him. 'You can't see anyone from this distance, Sweet.' She had booked this cottage in Burton-in-Lonsdale for the views, especially of the landmark mountain from the back kitchen window. 'My Ingleborough,' she called it.

'I can.' Ben took his finger away from the glass and made his hands into binoculars. 'They're climbing up the mountain.'

We all went to the kitchen window to see if he was right. 'Perhaps he's got super-sight,' I said.

My husband, David, rubbed his hands together. 'So is the Wensleydale plan still a go? We pack a picnic and see if we can get up as far as Aysgarth?'

'No.' Lori turned back to the table and began to pour the children's tonic into tiny measuring beakers. 'It's too far with Katie's teeth in this state. She's just going to grizzle in the car.' When she reached seven millilitres, she angled the tonic bottle upwards in time for the dribbling to stop precisely at ten. I had been watching this for five days, but it still entranced me. We used to just pour such things straight onto a medicine spoon with no precision at all. But I never say a word.

'Plan A dead on arrival! Never mind. On with plan B,' I said, my mind fizzing with the strain of tiptoeing through my words. 'Why don't we stay in Burton today? There's that lovely playing field with the swings.' I lifted Ben from his seat and put him next to Katie on the play mat. 'You'd like to go to the swings, wouldn't you, Ben?'

Ben emptied the contents of his doctor's bag and pushed a fake needle into my bare arm. 'You've got lots of blood pressure.' He pushed harder and twisted and I pretended to faint before making a dramatic recovery.

'Ben, you're a marvel. You've saved Granny's life.' I produced two pieces of shortbread like a magic trick and held them out to the children. Katie took one and passed it to her brother. 'Ah, look! Katie's giving it to you. She's so kind.'

'I'm kinder,' said Ben.

Lori let out a sharp sigh and swept the biscuits out of their hands and into the bin. 'This is *exactly* it!' she hissed to James, my son. 'It's far too early in the day!'

I stared at the swinging bin lid as Katie's wail poured into the shock. When I looked across at James, he was staring at it too; he did not meet my eyes.

Ben dropped his stethoscope. 'But that was mine!'

I stood up. *It was a bit of sugar, that's all. Not arsenic.* 'I'm

12

just going for a little walk.'

I got through the door a moment before my tears began. Again. Ben and Katie's only memory of me will be as a slack-faced red-eyed creature.

I suppose I must have looked a sight. I'd been awake for what felt like a long day already, and it could scarcely have been nine a.m., but by the time I reached the village shop I'd got myself under control. I bought a newspaper, then walked up to the church, intending to leave things to calm down.

A grey cat sat on one of the gate posts in front of the church porch. It jumped down and trotted up to me expectantly, then turned away before I could pet it, as if disappointed. It headed off round the corner of the church, looking at the house on the hill for a long moment, until I finally caught up with it and reached down for a stroke.

This pattern continued. The cat walked on, stopped and stared at something I couldn't see, as cats do; I followed it, stroking when I could and looking at all the same spaces, trying to see those elusive things it saw. It jumped onto the wide stonework of the church wall and bounced from level to level as we made our way downhill, arching its back and doing sideways skitters. I smiled. The newspaper stayed under my arm, unread. It was easy, following this cat; the easiest thing I'd done all week.

It had been my idea for all of us to come away together. Was that so wrong? I tried to arrange things so that *both* couples were running the holiday cottage, but it wasn't easy. Lori raced around doing everything.

'She needs to be in control,' David maintained.

'Let me help,' I would say. 'You sit down.'

She'd give me that tolerant but doubtful smile, her head on one side. And when I came down in the early mornings hoping to start breakfast, she would shift the baby around on her knee and sigh, as if I were intruding. And I was. I know that early morning time with your little one, when all the world is still asleep. Feels like yesterday. So I'd stopped doing that. I do listen, you see. I'm not one of those marauding mothers-in-law you read about on the parenting forums, the hated harridans who burst into delivery rooms or feed the grandchildren e-numbers. But bedtimes weren't available to me either, because Lori was a stickler for particular routines. James would do the baths and Lori read the stories one night, and then they would swap over.

The cat and I reached the huge church wall on Leeming Lane, so strong and straight where you'd expect it to bulge against the weight of all that soil. The cat sat and stared at that wall for ages, purring loudly. I started to feel calmer.

James and Lori argued about the most surreal things. I tried to tell them that these were the Baby Days and they would get through them—David and I got through them and we had some real blazers!—but sometimes I'm not so sure. I like my daughter-in-law, I really do, but the other day when James was wavering with a box of cling film and she told him to 'Put it back in the drawer it came from, because that'll be a new adventure for you' I couldn't just stand there. I had to help him tidy up.

'Let's just get going and leave all this till tonight,' I said.

That's not interfering, is it? When I think back to the way I used to treat David when James was little... but we'd had nobody to overhear us. How ashamed I'd be now, if we had. You come to your senses, you see, when the effects of the sleep deprivation wear off.

David was blithe, as always. 'You can't tell them. They have to find these things out for themselves.'

But he's my only son. It's so hard. You never stop wanting to protect them. Never.

How far would I go with this cat? *To the top of Ingleborough*, I thought, looking across at the mountain, at the beige and light purple of it in the sunshine on that first real spring day. I could follow it that far even in these shoes. I'm only fifty-eight. I could tell them I wasn't able to help it, that the cat was like some kind of Pied Piper. I looked at my watch: half an hour had passed already, but everyone deserves a break, surely? Don't you need a break from even the most precious things? The tension seemed to permeate everything on the breakfast table and the little ones ate breakfast so *slowly*. I swear, Ben was only four, but he seemed to eat five courses: Ready Brek, then toast, then Rice Krispies, then more toast, then a banana. Katie ate less, being only thirteen months, but she wasn't much faster.

At the crossroads where Chapel and Leeming Lanes meet, the cat yawned, showing youthful pink gums and clean teeth. It stared at a bird on a telephone wire, its jaws trembling, its whole body straining painfully, then streaked down Burton Hill like the wind. I followed sedately. I'd cried so much by this point in the holiday that I think I was almost all cried out. You learn pretty early on with a daughter-in-law that you have to take all she throws at you and that she is holding a sword of Damocles above your head. Well, now she had cut the horsehair thread. They were moving to Edinburgh, and had told us on our first night in the cottage.

'We could move too!' I'd whispered to David when we were in bed. Ben and Katie had fallen asleep early, so I still wasn't sure of the upstairs acoustics. 'We could. It's possible...'

But David insisted they needed their independence. 'They've got their own lives,' he said. 'We can't follow them wherever they go. It's their choice.'

I'd follow James and little Ben and Katie to the ends of the earth. I think I said as much to David, but he kept shaking his head. 'We can visit,' he said.

But it's not the same. It's never the same.

Katie's first steps were only a few weeks ago and even during this holiday her walking had grown bolder and steadier. Imagine missing things like that! I knew that Lori was only brittle because of the relentlessness of parenthood, but what memories to take from our last holiday! And I knew that James didn't always pull his weight, which made her cross—I didn't blame her one bit —but moving hundreds of miles away... how would we manage to see enough of the children? There was already an implication that I phoned them too often.

The cat sat on a patchwork piece of pavement halfway down the hill, allowing me space to admire the houses clinging to the hillside while it washed one back leg. Then it got up and tried to climb a dilapidated cardboard box, but its claws didn't catch and it slid comically down the sides. This triggered an image of Ben skating across the tiled kitchen floor in his socks at six a.m., Lori tetchy, the baby and me delighted.

'Never mind,' I murmured, scratching the cat behind its ear. This was a cat that liked to sit on everything. *Perhaps when you're a cat, that's the only way to make things your own.* I could relate to that. Your grandchildren are different. They're yours, but they're also someone else's, someone you can't second-guess, someone you have to trust. David doesn't feel it in quite the same way. He's trusting and accepting, even when Forsters Canning made him redundant three years before he was due to retire. Philosophical, that's David. Drives me mad.

I had passed nobody on the streets so far. Blissfully peaceful, this village, apart from the odd lorry thundering through. Lori used to come here as a little girl; there's some family connection. That's why we were here.

Just before the river bridge the cat turned right, leading me along a lane we'd yet to explore on this holiday. Beautiful woodland scene. Lucky people, whose houses lined this lane. The cat walked to the end and stopped in front of some gates leading to a waste water treatment plant that I'd never have known existed. It purred and wound around my legs. Easy ecstasy. I gazed around me. An almost vertical field rose between the valley floor and Leeming Lane with the church looming majestically behind it. *Imagine sledging down that piste if you were four...*

Then the cat had another change of heart and doubled back towards the village, darting up a side road and showing me more of the hillside-clinging houses. *Showing me... the houses....* It sat, of course, but the house wall it sat upon had a For Sale sign next to it. I stopped dead; the cat looked back at me and waited, and it seemed like an omen. Thinking about ways of staying here... yes, I was, and I hadn't yet let David in on my thoughts. The Lunesdale area is halfway to Scotland for us. They wouldn't be able to accuse us of following them then—not quite.

The cat didn't let me linger long. It was off, and I couldn't do anything but follow, so I bookmarked the house and we retraced our steps—Burton Hill, Leeming Lane, the church—while in my mind I practised phrases of persuasion:

If we stay in Stroud, we'll be the relatives who come to stay every so often...

They'll be shy *with us...*

But a three- or four-hour journey, on the other hand...

We continued past the church and along the curving lane back to the main road, with its beautiful parallel, sweeping hedge. I followed almost without thinking, my eyes focused on its tail held high and rude, my brain churning, chuntering, planning. We had almost run out of village before I came back to full consciousness. The cat sat down abruptly, curling its tail around its front legs in perfect china-cat pose. This time, the sitting-down seemed comfortable. Final.

'Oh,' I said. 'Is this the end of the road?'

It narrowed its eyes patiently, as if I'd just told a feeble joke and it was indulging me.

We had come to the school gates. When James was a toddler and prone to making a run for it at every opportunity, I used to see such places and wonder how they kept them in there without chains and guards on the doors. But at this school, on this day, there were mannequins at the windows. I say it again: there were *mannequins*, at every window, arranged as if they were about to do something athletic.

While I looked at the windows—round windows, arched windows, square windows, just like a child's drawing—the cat must have uncurled itself, because it streaked up the school yard and disappeared round the back. *Any minute now*, I thought, *it will appear in that little round window in the rafters, and that will put the lid on things.*

I looked around. Everything was so still. The gate wasn't locked so I started to walk up the yard. Of course, mannequins always seem to be looking right at you, but the one in the football strip with its forehead leaning against the glass really seemed to see me. I laughed aloud, delighted at the trouble the villagers must have gone to, but it felt odd to laugh alone, without even the cat to hear me. In fact, it felt so odd that I stopped walking well before I reached the windows. In the field across the wall, a low breeze blew the grass into rippling patterns; that and my breathing were the only movements.

Lori used to be a window dresser. I could picture her face when she saw this, and the children's faces. I could see us all laughing together.

I was glad to turn and walk away, to hurry back to the cottage and tell them all about it—but when I arrived no one was there. Had I really been that bad? I thought Lori might tell her virtual friends all about me, the ones from the parenting website James said she chatted on late at night, from what she called her 'prison'—but that was all. I looked around, but there was no note.

'Hello?'

You think about accidents and children being rushed to hospital, don't you? I stepped outside and saw that our cars were still in the drive. Wouldn't I have heard an ambulance? My breathing grew faster. Had they gone for a walk? Were they looking for me?

Sometimes, when you've lost something, if you go away and start all over again—begin again—it cures it. I've done that with wallets and keys. Once, it even worked for a seemingly intractable computer problem. I thought, *When I reboot in the morning, this virus, this glitch, will be gone.* And it was. I think of it as a kind of prayer. So I left the house and went around the block again. Up Low Street, round the corner to Duke Street and onto High Street. I glanced back at Ingleborough from there; it looked prehistoric. Lori's mountain.

I carried on up to the back of the church. I hung around there, looking at things the cat had seen, thinking about Ben's face when his biscuit disappeared. I willed a new beginning again, the eradication of all their moving plans—but it wasn't the same without the cat and anyway, that sharp, exciting early morning had melted away into mid-morning ordinariness.

18

And when I returned, there they all were in the kitchen. James had Katie on his knee and was running his hands up and down her back as if soothing wind. Lori was buttering sandwiches, leaning against the worktop with her weight on one hip, tired around the eyes, shattered in fact. David was sitting at the table with a cup of tea and the paper—an identical paper to the one I was still clutching. They looked like they'd never been away.

'Where've you been?' I asked. My voice was hoarse.

James lifted his head. 'Mmm?'

'I came back about fifteen minutes ago and none of you were here.'

James frowned and shook his head. 'Dad and I went to the shop with the kids. Lori's been just here, Mum. We're waiting for you.'

I stood in the kitchen doorway, trying to keep very still. I'd shouted through the house... hadn't I? Had she hidden upstairs? Had she been asleep? 'You'll never guess what I've just seen up at the school,' I said calmly.

James jiggled Katie on his knee.

'Mannequins, loads of them, at all the windows.' I didn't mention the cat. I didn't think it would help my case.

'Do you know what?' said Lori. 'This village used to be called Black Burton.'

I waited. Had she heard what I'd said? I swallowed. 'Mannequins!' I waited again. 'You'd appreciate them, Lori. In all these different poses, like something supernatural.' I came into the room properly and slipped the newspaper into the wood basket. They all carried on reading, sipping, soothing, buttering. Katie gave a high-pitched squeak and Ben covered his ears.

David finally lifted his head from the paper. 'You okay, Julia? You look as if you've lost a shilling and found sixpence!'

Then James said, 'The models must be part of that pageant.'

I looked at him and frowned.

'The village pageant... an Easter thing. The school kids were involved in making some kind of tableau, like the scarecrows in that other village on the way to Lancaster. You know? We managed to miss the whole thing. We were talking about it the other night, Mum.'

'Were we?'

Ben made his way over to Lori and pulled at her skirt. 'What's a mankin?'

Lori twisted from the waist down, her hands smeared with butter and coleslaw. 'Stop it Ben.'

'It's a dummy from a shop window,' I said, then walked across and swept Ben up into my arms. 'Come to Granny.' I nuzzled into his hair. Only five more days of this left. 'Black Burton?'

'It used to have a lot of potteries,' Lori said, 'and they made loads of smoke. There were coal seams, and at one time, it had about seven million pubs and a rough reputation.'

James looked strained and preoccupied, as if they had all been talking about something much more pressing before I came back. 'And Burton-in-Lonsdale has a panther, apparently,' he said.

David and Lori both turned their heads to look at him.

'I overheard some kids talking outside the shop. A panther. Lives in the woods. Been here for years.'

Nobody spoke for a while. Katie wrestled on James's knee until she'd worked her way down to the ground.

'Glad you went for a good long walk,' David said eventually. 'It should help with the sleeping thing.'

'Don't you want to come and see these mannequins?' I felt hot and my voice was cracking. 'Silly for me to be the only one who's seen them.'

Ben wriggled down from my arms and I crouched down beside him. 'They're really funny, Ben. Funny faces that look at you, like statues, all in different positions.' I pulled a face and lifted my arms up into a pose. 'You'd like to come and see the funny dummies, wouldn't you? With Granny?'

I pulled myself into a chair and Ben looked at me. I said, 'We could go up together. You, me and Katie. Give Mummy and Daddy a little rest.'

Lori glanced at James. David concentrated hard on a paragraph, his finger tracing his place on the page. Then Lori opened the fridge door and frowned at a six-pack of baby yoghurts. 'We need to get going with this picnic if the kids are to actually eat it,' she said. 'Otherwise it'll be all snacks and rubbish again.'

I couldn't see her face for the acres of thick dark hair that spilled down over it, but I can still remember the tone of absolute finality in her voice, tired as it was.

I watched James as Katie crawled away from him. He looked as if he'd like to get down on his hands and knees and crawl away too, and I felt a pang for him. The same pang as when I left him for his first full day at nursery all those years ago, and he'd turned to me with a look that said, *Is this really going to happen?* I shut up about the mannequins.

I kept the house I'd seen to myself—and my fingers crossed —and the rest of that day passed at the playing fields and the idyllic river, ending with a lovely meal out in Kirkby Lonsdale in the evening.

Needless to say, my wish didn't come true. Wish? Prayer? Anyway, it's all done and dusted now. They've gone, and wouldn't even let us help with the packing or the moving vans.

'Wait till we settle,' they said when David rang them last night. 'Give us a good couple of months.'

On their own, they mean, before we descend. But it's hard. Little Ben's front tooth gap will be gone in no time. Little changes, times you never get back. And the move to Burton-in-Lonsdale was vetoed. David isn't ready to sell the family home and leave his wonderful garden. Not yet, at least. So here we are.

James once told me that you can't read in dreams. The part of your brain that's used for reading isn't active during sleep, so you can't actually read any text. But when I go back to Burton-in-Lonsdale in my dreams, when I go around that block again and again in my efforts to reboot, I can read the signs quite clearly. *Low Street. Duke Street. High Street. Leeming Lane.*

Like the Tide

Sarah Dobbs

I'm here again, drawn back to the prom like a magnet, long after you're gone. But that's not true, I'm not compelled, I'm here for different reasons. This is the place we 'courted', that word your parents used sharing a secret couple-smile as they watched us over cous cous, vegetarian pizza, sugar-free non-alcoholic wine and non-dairy cheesecake. I almost miss them, and their hope for us, more than you.

I didn't care about the water though, something you thought was majestic. I didn't care about or remember the places you pointed out over that dark expanse, I cared about the fact that me and you made this prom magical, that we bickered over whether the statue, lit by blue fairy lights, was really Eric Morecambe or not. I was sure it was, that he was some sort of patron saint who had been born here. And you gave me a heavy-lidded look that said, *patron saint?* On the plaque, we discovered that Eric had just changed his real surname to match the town. Our laughter echoed on the concrete, up and down the prom, the deserted shop fronts and one fount of light and activity that was the single amusement arcade open. The laughter followed us, chasing, as we explored.

I'm stood here again, thinking of that laughter. Same prom, same concrete, same time of year. It's the sort of laughter you have before you stop being polite. I hear it differently now. Now, I can imagine reality tracking, us crumbling and you being gone. But I see everything differently now, your parents' faces, their reserved hope. Will this one be the girl that lasts?

There is a new man at my side and he squeezes my hand. He has long, thin fingers whereas yours were thick and hard to hold. Holding your hand hurt. I had to spread my fingers too wide.

'Have you ever been here before?' he asks.

He's tall with soft, falling hair and an interest in me that I want to look away from. 'Once,' I say.

And he knows why, I can tell.

'I thought it would be fun,' he says. 'Not exactly romantic though, is it?'

I'm supposed to help him out here, flirt and be placating: *Don't be silly,* or something. I shrug.

So we walk because I don't feel like talking, because I can still see the ghost of us sitting on those benches, you daring me towards the shoreline, the dog I patted, the bookshop we explored, stroking the shelves and the dust and the covers, you dreaming of moving somewhere near water, someday, and me implicitly included. But that was always the problem, the implicit, the tossed promises, the never-quite-real.

'I've always wanted to live by the water,' the tall guy says.

I close my eyes briefly. It's all so familiar, so pointless, but looking at the water I was sure I could construct a metaphor to convince me that this is just life, it's cyclical and people come and go. *Just like the tide* rings in my head. I roll my eyes. How corny. My hands suddenly detach from the tall guy. I don't know

24

whether it was me who let go, or whether I just wasn't holding on enough.

'What's up? Something funny?' He tickles me and the action is so unexpected I forget myself and laugh. I imagine this laughter painting over those old memories, that other beginning. It's been so long since you were gone. I miss how like children we were, the addiction of your spur-of-the-moment ideas, and yet, isn't that part of the reason you're no longer in my life? I was too all about the future.

I should take part in this date. I look at the tall guy and he meets my eyes, he thinks it's a moment, when really I'm just investigating; is this a face I could like? Can I love this face in the morning, when it's drunk, when it's angry, when we're making up? Can I see any point in this face? I smile, his coat is nice. I quite like how it crowds around his jaw.

'I like your coat,' I say.

I can see that interested-in-me face again and it churns my stomach. He finds me amusing and different, I think. Probably cute. I can imagine him thinking, *She likes my coat*. His spine seems to lengthen out with pride. The affect of my effect is kind of intriguing. My smile is less forced.

'Shall we go and look at the statue?' He raises his eyebrows, initially pleased with his idea, and then his face drops.

I imagine this is a glimmer of how he will look when he is much older, that slackness to his face. I expect more distaste, a physical reaction in me to keep us apart, but instead I just think that his features might pull off age fairly well. You couldn't call him handsome as such, well, not pretty in that way men seem to be these days, but I suppose it's a bold face. He suddenly reminds me of a man built of shale and rock, eroding with the years like the pebbles under the bay. I thrust out my lip, thoughtful.

'Penny for them,' he says.

God.

'Not telling?'

I shake my head. 'Let's go and look at the statue then.'

'You haven't seen it before?'

I don't answer and he seems happy to leave it that way.

25

There are still some days I can't believe you're gone and I wonder at the point of grinding on and meeting new people who aren't you. Except, with you, I just couldn't breathe.

I'm struck by a thought. 'Actually, let's go down onto the beach.'

I dive towards the steps but the tall guy takes his time. I'm half disappointed, remembering you dashing after me, beating me towards the water, my lungs icy and tight; the realisation that this with him is just not and never will be the same. But does that matter so much? Could that be good? I turn my back and grab a handful of sand. It's damp and clogs through my fingers and even when it's fallen, it's still on me. It's gritty between my fingers, making the movement of them less fluid. I reel in a lungful of salty air. It tastes wet and dark. I narrow my eyes at the night sky, like I'm looking into bright sunlight. It seems somehow brilliant and blinding.

The sand reminds me of our whole relationship, of me trying to just be and you seeming to want to hold me back, all that complexity. I thought about the water and whether the sand slowed its progress, tethering it from its natural impulse, or whether it was the other way around; the water smoothed over the earth, suffocating it. Were all relationships such a battle, this tussle for dominance, or could there ever be some sort of balance?

I look at the blackness beyond the water, the shapes that are blacker than the night, the sound of the water shrugging back and forth. Mystery and possibility. I clap and rub my hands together, knocking away as much of the sand as possible. Despite the early days, I am glad you are out of my life. I breathe in and out, again and again, realising just how easy it is now.

The tall guy stands by my side. I like that I rushed and he took his time. That maybe I can be myself and so can he, and that will be okay. I won't need to be different, to be someone else, because I, just me, would be enough.

'Andrew?' I say.

He looks at me, waiting.

'Statue?'

'Great. Do you think it's Eric Morecambe?'

'Only one way to find out,' I say and we start walking, me breathing in and out, like the tide.

Paper Cut
Clare Weze Easterby

They asked me to make a man for Aunty Heidi, so that's what I did.

It didn't take me long. I decided to do her a man in black, because then he'd be eye-catching and sophisticated and I could give his jacket straight, square shoulders. I drew him on cardboard and cut him out in seconds. Modelling clay would have been too heavy and I had a feeling she wanted someone bendy. I stuck a paper face on, coloured his hair in black felt pen, and gave him long, delicate paper hands, which made him look quite real.

There was just one thing I wasn't satisfied with: his hair still looked like felt pen. I ran across to the beach and found the perfect material straight away: seaweed. Black, washed up that morning and all dried out. Back at home, I snipped it into short strands and glued it on. It worked! Now his hair looked like it was flowing, even growing. The felt pen had been too flat, but this hair looked as if he'd just washed it. I took a sniff. Yes, you

29

could still smell seaweed, but it was fresh. I almost didn't want to give him up, but I took him round to her flat just as the sun was sitting perfectly on the watery horizon across the bay. A Morecambe man made with real Morecambe seaweed.

'Wow, that was quick! And what a man!' she said. 'He's magnificent! Just what I need. Thank you, Natalie.'

'Why do you need a man, Aunty Heidi?' Mum had said it was because she was lonely, but I didn't quite believe that; she's always had loads of friends. There was some kind of tangle between Mum and Aunty Heidi though—they hadn't quite fallen out, but they weren't exactly huggy-huggy sisters any more either.

'I need someone to mend my washing machine,' she said. 'And shave a fraction off the bottom of my front door to stop it sticking.'

'Dad can do things like that.'

'Yes... well, I think I need to stop bothering your dad.'

I looked at my cardboard man. He sat in Aunty Heidi's palms, his white face cradled against her thumb, his fingers spread delicately, as if he was just about to play the piano. They didn't look like strong, mending fingers. I was worried for Aunty Heidi. 'Can't you just phone the washing machine shop?'

She didn't answer me. She studied the man in her hands as if she, too, was wondering what he could do. Then she propped him between her teacup and a jar of honey, buttered our toast, as usual, and asked me about my day. The man seemed to smile across the table at her. After tea I sat on her window sill looking at the sea and the stone cormorants in the front garden, which Aunty Heidi always says make her feel like flying away over the sea.

Our house is next door to Aunty Heidi's, so when she went out the next day wearing a pale green dress I'd never seen before, with her hair up in a clip, I jumped down from the window and raced after her. She had a short, fluffy jacket over her shoulders and looked soft and touchable.

She was quite a way ahead of me, so I shouted her name, but my voice was drowned out by a motor bike. There were people on the beach, soaking up the last of the sun, as if it might

30

never come again. They looked funny compared to Aunty Heidi, all dressed up. So I kept following and didn't shout again. I felt a bit sneaky but I carried on doing it anyway.

I followed her all the way to the Midland Hotel. We live just behind the Battery right next to the sea just past where those new squirty water features are, so it's only up the road from us, and I'm allowed to go that far as long as I don't cross the road. She went inside. This was so weird. Aunty Heidi always tells me if she's going somewhere special. Why had she kept this secret?

I watched her disappear through the big glass doors, then ran up to them and peered through. I'd been in once before; the whole family came when it first re-opened. I stepped inside and stood next to a leaflet stand, my heart beating like mad in case anyone saw me, in case Aunty Heidi turned around... but she didn't.

She stopped in the middle of the floor beneath the circular staircase. There were lots of people; my ears rang with the buzz of their chatter. Then a man came up to her. I didn't see where he came from; he was just suddenly there, jangling his keys in his pockets as he walked. Aunty Heidi turned to him and they held hands for a second. Blink and you'd have missed it. He was dressed in black, like my cardboard man. Black trousers, black shirt, black shoes… and dark hair! I gasped out loud—I couldn't help it—so then I had to shrink farther back behind the leaflet stand in case she heard me even through all the burbling voices.

They moved off and I followed. They went right through to the Rotunda Bar, got some drinks and took them to a table near the window. I stood in the doorway near the top of the basement stairs and looked into the amazing round room with its glass wall, like the one in Aunty Heidi's flat, and its chandelier. Aunty Heidi has one of those too. The whole hotel could almost *be* Aunty Heidi's flat, but about a hundred times bigger. A waitress glided around carrying a tray loaded with cups and cakes. She moved across the floor smoothly, like a robot. I smelt coffee and new decorating and perfume. And I looked at the two of them at the window, and I couldn't believe it.

Aunty Heidi looked excited. She smiled a lot more than

31

usual. She talked, and smiled as she talked, showing her teeth. I wished I was close enough to hear what they were saying. What could they be saying? She looked a bit stiff, as if she was doing something difficult. Then he went back to the bar for more drinks and I got a better view of him: he was young, tall and thin with a pale face, just like the man I'd made. Perhaps if he'd been wearing jeans, or if he hadn't been so tall... but no, he was dressed exactly as I'd made him.

Someone stopped beside me. 'Can I help you?' It was the gliding robot waitress. My heart thumped like mad.

'It's okay,' I said. 'I'm just waiting for my aunt.'

The waitress smiled and glided away with her tray, but I thought I'd better move around a bit, so I went downstairs and wandered through the massive bathroom and sat on some sofas and pretended I was famous. By the time I'd got back to my doorway, the man had sat down again and this time, he was leaning right over Aunty Heidi and all I could see of her was a little sprig of red hair poking out from the top of his black head. He must have bewitched her. What can you talk about that's so important you have to get close up like that? And if my cardboard man had come to life, then he probably *did* have strange powers. Should I rescue her? Should I walk across to them and pretend Mum wanted her for something?

I looked at the back of his head as he nodded, again and again, as his shoulders shrugged up and down, as his hands brushed something from his trousers, then brushed again as though sand was clinging to them. I tried to make out the strands of seaweed-hair. If I did walk up to them, I'd be able to see the seaweed. I'd be able to touch it. I'd know.

I went outside. I walked right round to the back, where the Midland looks out across the sea. I thought if I crept up to the window, Aunty Heidi would have her back to me and I could get a good look at his face, and if he recognised me—well, that would prove it, wouldn't it? But when I got there, I realised that everyone else would be able to see me too, and I'd look suspicious. So I sat on the little wall where the railings loop round and round, and watched from there. I'd picked up a leaflet on the way out and I held it in front of my face, pretending to read. I squinted to get a better focus on his eyes—I had drawn beautiful eyes on that white paper—but it was still too much of a blur through the glass, and he kept looking in my direction. I wished I hadn't given him a black shirt. I should have given him a pink one with frilly cuffs. I should have given him blonde hair, or afro hair, not that black seaweed that was making me feel creepy.

I watched them for ages, until I started to feel as if I just couldn't look any longer. I stood up and scanned the sea; the tide was miles away. I ran along the prom towards home, but I didn't really want to go there. My best friend Megan was away in Greece all summer, otherwise I'd have been straight round to her house. The traffic crawled along both lanes beside me. I looked at the sand and the people and I looked at the white sky and I thought, *What am I going to do?*

At home, Mum was on the computer, but I didn't let that stop me. 'Mum! Aunty Heidi's with a man in the Midland Hotel!'

'What? How do you know?'

'I've seen her. And he's dangerous! He's not a real man! He's a thing!'

'A thing? What do you mean, a thing? Anyway, it's none of our business who Aunty Heidi sees and where she sees him. Don't be nosy.'

'No, it's that man I made for her—you know, *the man*! He's come to life!'

But of course, Mum just laughed. 'Tell 'em tall, tell 'em all, tell 'em to the wall,' and I got nowhere with her.

I went to Megan's house and fed her rabbits. I took my time and gave them a one-handed stroke while they sat side by side nibbling their grains. I was slow and careful, because they try to burst out of the cage door if you don't hold it tight. Then I raced round to Aunty Heidi's, but she still hadn't come home. I tried again just before bedtime, but there was still no sign of her.

When she came home from work the next day I was waiting on her doorstep. I asked her about the man all the way up the stairs to the flat. 'I saw you through the window in the Midland. He's your boyfriend, isn't he? Why didn't you tell me

33

you had a boyfriend?'

She shook her head and laughed at me. *'Dream a little dream of me,'* she sang from her bedroom as she swapped her white dental nurse's uniform for a summer dress.

'Where did you find him?' I shouted through.

'We just got talking, and we clicked.'

'But where?' I could hear her getting cross with the tangle of coat hangers in her wardrobe. 'Where?'

'Here, there, everywhere,' she said, coming back to sit with me. 'Just around. All around the place.'

'But that's like when I ask how old you are and you say, 'As old as my tongue and a little bit older than my teeth.''

'Yes,' Aunty Heidi giggled. 'And that's true too! It's the God's honest truth. No, really, I met him on the Lunesdale Studio Trail. I've signed up for a course in mosaics. He's a sculptor, and he's going to make a seahorse for my windowsill.'

I studied her face. People's eyes try to concentrate on something when they're lying, but her eyes just looked into mine and crinkled when she smiled, so I wasn't sure. Because just lately, Mum says Aunty Heidi makes it up as she goes along.

Suddenly, I thought of something. 'Where's the man?'

'What man?' she asked.

'The *man*. The man I made you.'

'Oh. He's on the bookcase, I think.' She got up and went over to look. 'Oh... perhaps not. Oh well, he's somewhere around.'

'Have you lost him?'

''Course not, Sweetheart. I treasure the things you make for me. He's probably in the bedroom.'

There wasn't anything suspicious in her voice or the way she looked, but I didn't believe her—not one word. 'I'll try to find him for you,' I said, and I wandered from room to room, feeling a little bit spooked, as if the man was here, secretly, and was playing a game with me.

I like Aunty Heidi's flat because it's so much tidier than our house, and calmer too. There's only Aunty Heidi living there, for one thing, and for another, whatever Aunty Heidi does in her place, Mum does the opposite in ours. I couldn't find the man.

Back at home, I pushed my food all around my plate instead of eating. 'The man I made her isn't there any more, and that man she met in the Midland is pretending to be a sculptor. He's tricking her. He's probably pretending he can help her with her mosaic classes.'

Mum looked up from her dinner. 'Mosaic classes?' she said. 'Since when did she decide to do mosaic?'

'I don't know. She's even told him that seahorses are her favourite creatures.'

Mum put her knife and fork down. 'I thought we were both going to do watercolours. That's what she said.'

'She met him at the Lunesdale Trail. It must be a walk through a wood.'

'No, it's an art thing... art studios. It's called the Lunesdale Studio Trail. So he could be anyone—a visitor, perhaps. But that doesn't mean he's tricking her, Natalie. You're getting carried away again.' She picked up her cup of tea and cradled it next to her mouth without drinking. 'Well, he'll know he's got her, that's for sure. What's his name, anyway?'

I gasped. 'She never said!' *I bet he hasn't got one! That's why!* I thought, remembering how small and neat he had looked in her hand when he was still cardboard. *Tinsy. Harmless looking.* But the most deadly octopus is only the size of a marble; Aunty Heidi had told me that.

Dad was already clearing away, saying nothing. I could tell he was listening though. You can always tell, can't you, even when someone has their back to you? His shoulders were stiff and he looked over at Mum every so often.

So I made some plans. I'd follow the man and find out where he slept and if he turned back into cardboard when he rested or when people weren't looking at him. I clicked through the Internet, looking for things that change. *Butterflies... frogs... metamorphosis*—wherever I clicked I found *metamorphosis*, but nothing quite like the man. I landed on a page with a beautiful picture of a dragonfly and remembered what Aunty Heidi once told me about them: they live for two years as a nymph underwater, then spend just one month as an adult above ground.

Like the man, perhaps? Just a month would be okay.

So all that week I looked out for him. On the beach, up and down outside the squirty water features, all around the new flats, at the fairground, even down the road towards Heysham village, which is further than I'm allowed to go. But I never found him on his own. No matter how I timed it, he always got to Aunty Heidi's flat without me seeing, so they were always together.

One day, after I'd given up trying to beat him, I decided to follow the pair of them. They turned right towards the Battery and I let them get almost to the flats before I set off. At first it went well. They didn't look back at all, so I got daring and by the time they'd reached the play area I was just behind them. This was the closest I'd ever been to him, and I could smell him. He smelt of cooking oil and Mars bars. I had to get even closer to hear what they were saying.

'And the devil take the hindmost,' Aunty Heidi said.

'Do you get me?' he said. His voice was low and croaky, like a crow.

I couldn't hear what Aunty Heidi said in answer to that, but next, she said, 'As long as nothing crops up.'

'That was real,' he said.

What was real? I couldn't understand them. His hair looked as if he'd polished it.

Then Aunty Heidi stopped and they both turned around suddenly. 'Natalie!' she said.

I jumped.

'Rod and I are just going for a little walk by ourselves.'

Rod? Huh! I refused to call him that, ever. To me, he was just *The Man*. And what on earth did they talk about all the time? He wouldn't know about any of those things Aunty Heidi liked to tell me—the dragonfly nymphs, the moons of Jupiter, how nettles sting you with tiny injection needles. He could only possibly be interested in greasy things. I was sure of it. I could tell by the way he smelled.

I didn't think Aunty Heidi would ever forget me. Mum and Dad go to see a film at the Dukes once a month, and drop me off at ballet first. Aunty Heidi always picks me up, takes me home and stays with me till they get back, as it's late and the house is empty. Or sometimes, we watch a film at her place. But one night she forgot. That night, she was too busy doing whatever it was she did with *The Man*, and I came out of ballet and waited next to the sweet shop... and waited.

After twenty minutes, I started walking. It's a long way back from Bare. Too long. At first it was like an adventure, as if the whole of Morecambe had been laid out for me to explore. I'm not allowed out after eight at night, and never beyond the Midland, not by myself.

On Bare Avenue, I found a pen in my pocket and ran it along wall tops, railings and hedges to listen to the different noises it made. I was almost happy. It felt so different; nobody knew where I was, and the street looked magical in the sunset, like a film or a dream. But that feeling didn't last very long. It's freaky, but it just seemed to tip over from one street to the next, because suddenly, I wanted to be home already. There weren't many people on Seaborn Grove, which made me feel like everyone knew a better way and was taking it. An old woman shuffled along in her slippers. She gave me the creeps. Then I saw an old-fashioned doll with stiff gold hair and a lacy dress just standing on its own in a window on New Market Street. It didn't look like it was supposed to be there; you could almost believe that it had just wandered out of a cupboard and was waiting for something to do.

Mum and Dad turn their mobiles off in the Dukes and Aunty Heidi usually sorts all that stuff out anyway. I felt loose, like a boat cast adrift. I headed for the sea. Aunty Heidi once said that the sign for Marine Road made her think she was on holiday, even though she's lived here all her life, so I thought it might make me feel better too. Then the wind got going, picking up crisp packets and takeaway boxes and hurling them into the street, and I was cold.

I expected to feel safe again when I came out of Seaborn Road. There was Marine Road. There was the beach, the sea, the big rocks, with perching seagulls. But I still felt like I was an awful event waiting to happen. Nobody was outside eating or drinking tonight. It was too blustery, and the only people around were gangs of staggering, swaggering lads. Too many lads, and I was too small, not even quite a teenager. I ran past them and found somewhere to cross the road, but I had to wait ages. At the other side there was a dog tied to some railings and going mad at nobody, everybody. I looked it in the eye as I passed, but that just seemed to make it worse.

The stone seagulls and cormorants and puffins that line the car parks and all the edges of things seemed safe, like nobody could ever hurt them and they'd still be there in a hundred years. The real seagulls hunched their wings up miserably against the wind. My lungs went all tight and my breathing felt squeezed. My coat blew forward and my hair flew high in the air, knotting up and stinging my eyes, so by the time I got home I looked icky and messed up and my lips tasted salty. Even the sea looked sulky and grey. The tide was in and the waves slumped against the concrete wall as if they wanted to slap somebody.

I reached the house at the same time as Mum and Dad, which was wrong, wrong, wrong.

'Where've you been?' said Mum. 'Where's Heidi?'

'She never turned up. She's probably with that man.' I glanced up at the dark windows of Aunty Heidi's flat.

'What?' Mum said, going inside and tugging at her jacket. 'She's left you to walk home on your own?'

'I told you I need a mobile.'

We all stood in the kitchen.

'My mother always said she'd push us past the giddy limit one day,' said Mum. 'Always.' I got an image of Granny when she was young, wagging her finger at naughty Aunty Heidi.

They stared at me. 'Are you all right?' asked Dad.

I nodded.

'Is that bloke leading her by the nose, or what?' said Mum. She looked funny just standing there in the kitchen, not moving, not doing anything, just fuming.

Then we heard the click of Aunty Heidi's garden gate, and a giggle.

38

'Right,' said Mum. She says that just before she does something important. *Right*. It means something is getting going. 'Right. I'm going round there.'

A horrible hot feeling swept through me. 'But what are you going to do? She just forgot.'

'June,' Dad said. 'You'll regret it. You know you will.'

'I don't care,' Mum said, and she left the house.

'What will she regret?' I asked, but Dad just shook his head and gave me the lot-of-fuss-about-nothing look, which I might have believed if his eyebrows hadn't given him away. They go up into little arrow heads when he's worried. I found a pen and drew loose eyebrows on his newspaper till Mum came back.

She made cheese on toast for supper. Dad stood back and let her do it. He didn't ask. She didn't tell. Everyone sat and ate cheese on toast thinking about Mum and Aunty Heidi and what might have been said, but nobody spoke. I made an arrowhead out of my knife and fork, carefully, without wobbling the table. I tried not to look at Mum in case she was an unexploded bomb that would only go off if you stared too long. She concentrated on her food, eyeing each piece as if she really meant what she wasn't telling it, and she didn't look at me either.

So then there was an even bigger rift between her and Aunty Heidi. It went on for weeks and weeks; I thought it was never going to end. And nearly every day there was the man, slipping up the stairs next door, and you only ever caught a glimpse of him—his back disappearing, or sometimes a side view —but always, a feeling came off him, a kind of gloating. It was as if he was glad about the argument because now he could have Aunty Heidi all to himself. I even saw him in the morning once. The week before term started again, I looked up at her window on my way to Megan's rabbits and he was standing there, his dark head filling the pane. He yawned when he saw me, as if he'd just woken up. It was the most awful yawn I've ever seen in my life. It went on for ages and was wider than a mouth should really be.

'Can we go bowling?' I asked Mum one day.

'I've got a lot to do. Maybe later.'

'You're all busy. Megan's on holiday and Aunty Heidi's with

39

that man.'

'Don't bother your aunt.'

'It's not like a summer holiday,' I said. A seagull squawked just outside our window.

Mum took hold of my cheeks in both hands and squeezed. 'That's the way it goes sometimes.' She looked all dreamy. 'Why don't you just go to the beach or play around the fountains? If you wait for other people to make your entertainment, you'll be waiting and waiting till Christmas has been and gone.' I had the feeling that she wasn't just talking about me.

I dreamt about how easy it would be to get rid of him. I could just throw him in the sea and watch him soak and float. In a while, he'd melt and disintegrate and get washed up with the line of froth. Or I could walk across the sands when the tide was out and bury him. Aunty Heidi's told me there are fields of gas under that sea. If I walked far enough out and dug far enough down, I could bury him on top of the sandstone where the gas is stored. I liked the idea of him being on top of a load of gas. Or I could just cut him into little ribbons and throw him in the bin... The only trouble was, I couldn't find him, could I? Not in his true, cardboard form, anyway.

'It's not the same now Aunty Heidi's got a man,' I moaned again.

'Natalie!' Mum looked just like Aunty Heidi when she was surprised. 'That isn't a very nice way to put it.'

'Well it's true. She's never here, and when she is, she's different.'

She didn't say I was right, but she didn't say I was wrong, either.

'She's all fuzzy and dreamy. Why does having a boyfriend make you go like that?'

Mum just shook her head and flashed her eyes to the ceiling, as if she had things to say but wouldn't join in.

I tried Dad, but he just said that Aunty Heidi was bound to meet somebody one day, that everyone did eventually.

'Maybe there are lots of cardboard men around,' I said, which got me thinking: Why just cardboard men? Why not

40

women too? And wouldn't a cardboard man be happier with a cardboard woman?

I didn't stop to think about all the possibilities; I just got my scissors out again. I made her blonde and as pretty as I could, which was easy because I've got lots of Clarice Bean books and there are some lovely faces to copy in those. I made her dress out of actual red velvet from an old cushion and stuck it on with super-glue. Her shoes were real Cinderella slippers made from a shiny blue plastic bag with mega-high heels. I got really into it. The heels were cut from a white yoghurt pot; I thought I'd better make them fairly sturdy.

I took it round to Aunty Heidi's with some biscuits I'd made. 'Has it come to this, Petal?' Dad teased, but I was glad. The biscuits would get me in—me and the cardboard woman.

'Back to school soon,' said Aunty Heidi.

The Man didn't speak at all, and he ate none of my biscuits. I glared at him. *Dragonfly*, I thought.

'You'll be glad to see Megan again.' Aunty Heidi rubbed her hands together and cleared our cups and plates away. She looked as if she was in a hurry to wash up.

I hid the cardboard woman in the bathroom window behind a spare loo roll. And it was odd, because as soon as I'd put her in position, one of those thin spindly spiders began to spin round and round on its web in a corner near the ceiling. They don't usually do that unless you touch them.

It didn't take long. I saw the two of them together—the cardboard man and the cardboard lady—in that café in front of the Battery just three days later on a rainy teatime. Her glass slippers looked solid enough now. The waiter who served them kept saying, 'It's not a problem,' at the end of every sentence. His voice was loud, as if he thought they might be deaf.

'Four chocolate chip cookies to take away, please,' I said. I was sure the man would look across when he heard my voice, but he didn't. Perhaps he was just pretending not to listen. Outside, seagulls screeched and swooped over the wet sand. After walking a little way, I looked back over my shoulder and thought I saw them both staring after me. *It's not a problem.* The words stayed in my mind all the way home.

'I told you he'd be a fly-by-night,' said Mum, when we found out Aunty Heidi was on her own again.

'When did you say that?' I asked, but neither Mum nor Dad wanted to talk about Aunty Heidi or her ex-man. They did have her to tea though, for the first time in months.

Mum grumbled about the only type of bread that had been left in Tesco's, and then raved about the cakes in the Italian market. 'They're magnificent!' and the rice at the new Nepalese stall, 'You have to watch them or they persuade you into all kinds.' But I could tell she was trying her best.

Aunty Heidi was wary, but agreed as hard as she could. 'You have to stop them piling chutney into the small tubs and squashing it down. Before you know it, you've parted with ten pounds.'

The room felt a bit strange because nobody mentioned *The Man*, but everyone was thinking about him, and it felt like it might start raining on us any second, even though we were in the kitchen.

'We could go bowling again now,' I said to Aunty Heidi.

She looked down at her hands for a moment. 'That would be fun, Natalie.'

'You'll get all the strikes,' I told her, to cheer her up, and she smiled at me but her eyes stayed sad and sort of worn out.

I'd been back at school for nearly a month before she started laughing properly again, and taking me to places, showing me things like she used to. She wasn't fuzzy and dreamy any more, but she wasn't quite the same as she'd been before I made that man, either. Never quite the same again.

Pop
Kay Douglas

Many years later, I sat implanted in the lining of the old Odeon as a rack of blitzed homes flickered on a newsreel. A sense of longing tugged me into that bombed-out street with all the remaining triangles of floor, wall and stairs. Up there in black and white was proof of what I'd always known: the cupboard under the stairs was the safest place in any house.

My brother, Lawrence, 'Pop', as I always refused to call him, could have got into the cupboard easily, but he was more interested in squirming out of places – scuttling up yard walls, shinning over railings, dropping from the bedroom window, onto the scullery roof and away.

Me too, that little cupboard door led to anywhere but our house. There were dark green jungles in there, rain hissed like spit bouncing off the flat iron. There were bullies, swindlers, snobs and a hundred miles of frozen tundra to span. On one occasion it had been full of gun smoke, caught in the crossfire of

45

the fourteenth of July 1789. But to Pop it was just a blur of dark wood as he shot out of the front door, into the light.

He tore through our lives did Pop, with no more feeling than the twister in 'The Wizard of Oz'. Once, he ran off with next doors' bike and I was sent to find him. From the bridge over the canal I saw Pop running on the towpath. His head was down as he wheeled the black, green and gold roadster at speed next to the water.

'Lawrence!' He stopped. Without looking at me, he let go of the handlebars and extended his fingers, like a magician. Three guineas worth of gents bike hit the canal with a crash of water and Pop creased into a helpless belly laugh; sounding like any other kid. Usually Pop was stern faced. When he threw rice pudding at the wall he concentrated his gaze on the stain as it soaked the parlour wallpaper, his lips clenched blue and white. Pages ripped out and screwed up from a library book were only interesting as the thin paper crinkled and uncrinkled. He once gave his shoes away. He left us all to land anyhow. He never meant any harm and I never meant to start imagining life without him.

One day, my mate Frank Salt stood at our back door. He had a football made of rolled up newspapers under his arm.

Mam said to me, 'Are you not taking your little brother, then?'

Frank's eyes begged me to pretend not to hear, but I always did. Pop slowly raised a stiff arm for me to put on his jacket. As we played, he stood alone for a moment in the back alley, but was soon surrounded. He got his nickname because kids would fizz him up to be rewarded with a geyser of swear words that, as Mam said, were not learnt at home. I stopped playing when I heard, 'Bugger off, you big bloody buggering buggers...' and sure enough, he erupted into a powerful sprint. Brandysnap ringlets sprang from the peaceful ginger waves Mam had soothed down and the wiry little legs pushed the ground away and we were off once more, like pictures caught in one of those spinning drums at the fair; a big lad chasing a little one. Pop was a fast runner and I was only any good at being good. I rounded a corner under a railway arch, gaining on him, passing a group of men. One shoved out a boot, hurling me chin-first into a cartoon skid along the grit of the road, 'That'll teach you then, won't it, you little bastard.' Justice done.

The more I fetched him home, the more he ran away. It didn't matter where I was – kicking a can in the street, sat in a classroom, or even at the pictures on a Saturday morning, they'd always find me, 'Kenny, your Pop's just done his nut and run off.' Somehow, everyone, including me, just accepted it was my job to find him.

Christmas came and I got a new torch. A six-inch chrome cylinder and funnel from F.W. Woolworth's, the sight of which had brought an instant rush of sweat and questions. Nothing on any of their faces told me anything. If they hadn't realized, then the betrayal was now greater but more enjoyable with each tiny, matt black letter more definite on brilliant white pages. This particular day I had waited until the hall was empty and then slid 'The £1,000,000 Pound Banknote' under a clammy pile of clean dusters along with a clutch of aniseed balls. For a ten-year-old, I was always keen for us to get us to bed on time.

'Mam, Dora and Theresa are fighting again. You're worn out you two. Yes you are, you're shattered. I might as well go up n'all. Come on then, and you, our Lawrence, that's it. Come on. Goodnight all.'

'You're playing a blinder there, our Kenny.'

Dad turned off the goblin shadow of the gaslight. I squinted a pillow-side eye at Pop lying next to me, eyes agape at the ceiling. I knew if I fell asleep, I'd be sure to wake up when Pop began his hammering snore. I never understood how that reedy rattle could blare from such little nostrils. I was three when Lawrence was born and had waited and waited for him to unfurl into a little boy that I could kick a football to. As I lay there, I thought about how it had turned out. He was always going to let the football roll to his feet and step away from it, as he did with words and glances. Lawrence, my little brother, who should have been swapping looks, whispers, trading cards and building dens with me had finally and forevermore done a runner, leaving this

47

'Pop' who left me smelling of his wee in the morning, took all my football playing teatimes and gave me nothing in return.

Frozen air crept round the curtains but there was no draught. Dad had nailed down the sash in the bedroom window after Pop's previous outings. The top of the front door was always bolted. When Pop closed his eyes I counted, as always, to two hundred and fifty, and then I was up and off. What Mam and Dad didn't know was that it was me who was the serial escapee.

By day, with all the clatter in the house I tested each stair, finding the quietest path. By night, I fancied myself as a soundless spirit hunter. I glided down stairs, scissored the black hall and spanned the ray of gaslight under the door to the kitchen, where Mam and Dad were listening to the wireless. Then, with a single movement – *open sesame* – I was curled in a dark hole upholstered with paraffin, camphor fumes and swollen newspapers. I positioned the torch beam and got as far away as I could.

I heard Mam and Dad go up to bed. I'd listened first to Dad's considerate footfall and then Mam's unapologetic tread above my head. My heartbeat slowed. I didn't know if I was in a cockpit or a womb. Had they never looked in the bedroom to see one of us missing? Or did they smirk as they passed the pool of torchlight under the little door? Henry Adams' adventure ended with him finding a wife and he returned the banknote intact. I had no idea how late it was.

When I got back up to the bedroom the air was sharp and frozen, the curtains fattened in an icy breeze; a slice of wood with nails in it swung from the sash. Inside the empty but still warm bed I watched as sleet spattered the closed half of the window.

'Don't come back,' I whispered, and drifted into a guiltless sleep.

The sleet hardened into snow. Dad and his brothers searched through two days and nights. Days in which I woke up dry and clean, stayed in school all day and played football with Frank and the others at teatime. On the third day I came in and Mam was by the fire, rocking a shape wrapped in a blanket. She was crying. He'd got as far as the Crook o' Lune, a farmer had found him huddled by a wall, 'like a cade lamb,' she said, remembering her childhood. I moved towards her. Mam kept rocking and as I got closer I could see Lawrence. His skin was pink. His eyes opened and turned towards me. I looked back at him, but we didn't swap anything.

Black Burton
Clare Weze Easterby

I have a small claim to fame, and it all began in the discos they used to run in the top room of the Joiners Arms in Burton in Lonsdale. People travelled from as far as, ooh, Caton and beyond for those discos.

One night there was a power cut in the middle of 'Video Killed the Radio Star'. I was with a real beauty. Ginny had come from one of those little hamlets near Kirkby Lonsdale and she had long, curly red hair lit up with flashes of gold from the disco search-lights, like a pre-Raphaelite, although I didn't know what such things were in those days. Anyway, she looked like an angel, she was smiley and full of fun, and I couldn't believe my luck. As soon as the music died and they started hunting for torches and candles behind the bar, I took her hand and we went out into the night. High Street was black below a moonlit sky, and it was quite warm for October.

'Spooky!' she whispered, and squeezed my hand. It was perfect. The world stopped dead and me and Ginny slipped

51

through the night.

Things have an odd slant in the dark. I was wondering whether I could take her into the church porch for a kiss when we came to a window with dozens of candles and people milling around a dinner table. There must have been mirrors in the room because the candles were reflected endlessly. We stopped and stared until Ginny started to shiver. Her flimsy, floaty dress was perfect for a stuffy disco but completely wrong for the night air, even a warmish night, and her jacket was just some insubstantial thing that matched the dress. So of course, I put my arm round her, along with my coat, and we carried on up towards the church like a real couple.

I was walking on air. It felt like the silence and the darkness were one and the same thing, and whatever it was had fallen on the village like a gift. Then we heard thunder towards Bentham and I realised what had knocked the power out.

The church rose up in front of us, a black silhouette, its spire looking longer than you'd believe. 'Where are we going?' she asked.

'There's seats in the porch,' I said, and I guided her in and down onto the cold stone bench. 'It's like a cave in this light.'

Our eyes got used to the deeper darkness and I turned to her, but she looked away shyly. For blokes, awkward moments like that are good opportunities to dive in, so I kissed her. It seemed to go down well. Her arms came up and wound around my neck and she returned the kiss.

'You're gorgeous, you,' I said. You've got to understand that the moon and stars were out and the street lights were off, and I might be a skip hire driver, but I'm soft inside. 'I could stay with you forever,' I said, meaning *in the moment*. I didn't mean what she must have taken it to mean.

She played her cards right out. 'I knew it was going to happen tonight,' she said. 'I knew I'd find the love of my life.'

And now things didn't feel quite so magical any more. Things felt awkward; I'd had a bit to drink, but not enough. I was only nineteen. Suddenly, those angel curls didn't look quite so attractive.

'It was meant to be,' she said, winding her fingers into my hair with her head on one side, her eyes all glassy. 'I think I've even dreamed of your face, Adrian.' She spoke very quickly; I had to concentrate quite hard to follow what she said.

'Steady down a bit,' I said, pulling away. Your mind scans back at moments like this. It rewinds to the beginning while you work out how you ended up at such a place. Before the power cut I'd been drifting a little. It was one of those nights when everyone is in tight little groups that you just can't break into and you rattle around the place like a buzzing bluebottle. I was a ripe target for Sam, the local alcoholic, but I managed to shake him off. Ginny was at the bar and her friend had just gone to the loo. I bought her a drink—something blue and sparkly like blue bols and lemonade. It was too loud to talk easily so we started to dance and then the lights went out and there we were.

'We've only just met,' I said, frowning at the smooth flagstones on the floor.

'But you can meet my mum tomorrow. You can come round for tea. We lost my dad last month, but my mum'll really love you.'

I was too young, back then, to know how death can affect people, but I knew I had to put her straight. I shifted away a little more, my trousers and jacket rustling in the darkness. I cleared my throat. 'I don't want anything heavy,' I said. 'I'm not ready to get involved.'

Her whole body went still and quiet. She looked at me, rosebud lips in a straight line, eyes dull with disbelief.

The next bit's muddled, because I stood up and turned away from that look. In fact, I don't even remember how she came to be out of the porch and climbing up the flagpole on the green—I really don't. But seeing her up there, obviously about to top herself, brought the taste of my last drink back up from my stomach and I rushed across the green.

'What the hell are you playing at?'

She didn't reply. I could hear nothing but my own jerky breath. I wrapped my arms and legs around the pole and started to pull myself up there, but it wasn't as easy as you'd think. It

53

takes all your strength just to keep clinging on, let alone
manoeuvre and support another body, especially when the mind
in control of that body is probably unhinged enough to dislodge
the pair of you at any second. I stopped just beneath her and
clung on with my aching left arm while my right stretched up
towards her. When I was sure of my grip I got hold of her round
the waist and tried to joke her out of it. 'Should've brought a
ladder out tonight!'

Unlike me, she didn't seem to be gripping on like a
desperate monkey. There was an athletic grace about the way her
legs folded around the pole, arms comfortable, loose even, and I
began to wonder whether she'd really intended to do away with
herself in this dramatic style in the first place.

Then the storm hit.

A thunderclap, and not too long after it, not nearly long
enough for my liking, an answering flash of lightning. 'Come on!'
I yelled. 'We're halfway up what may as well be a flaming
lightning rod!'

Then the wind came and blew hair into our eyes and there
was another flash. I felt a jolt, but it was nothing major. We both
slid down and landed in a stunned heap at the bottom of the
church green. We looked at each other in the moonlight. Her face
was blank, as if all the life had been sucked out of her.

'What was that?' I said stupidly. She didn't answer, so I
answered myself: 'It must have been the electric coming back on.
Look.' The street and house lights were twinkling again.

She was slack in my arms; it was like manhandling a rag
doll, and she may have been a delicately boned thing, but she was
tall. 'Come on,' I said, giving her a shake. 'We're going to get
cold. Let's get back to the Joiners.'

It took a couple of minutes and a bit of grunting and
pulling, but in the end she stood properly and we walked back to
the pub as the rain came. It felt bizarre to just stand at the bar and
wait to be served, as if nothing had happened. It felt preposterous,
like we'd been caught in some horrible act. The crowd had
thinned out and the lights seemed too bright, like lozenges with
rims that hurt your eyes.

I glanced at her. 'That must have been a power surge... or else the pole was struck by lightning.'

She didn't say a word; her lips were pursed. We stood there for a quite a while.

I held out my five pound note, but the bar staff ignored us. I waved my money. I stood up taller, I sighed, I fixed one of the bar staff with a stare and raised my eyebrows, but she just carried on clearing glasses and didn't meet my eye. It was as if I—we— were invisible.

'Are we dead?' I said to Ginny loudly, with a laugh, but she didn't laugh back. She didn't even smile. 'We've certainly got electrifying presence. Look how quickly they jump to it!'

Still she didn't react.

It must have been while I was clanging two glasses together to make a total racket that Ginny disappeared. I'd finally got served, so we weren't dead—or at least, I wasn't—but she was nowhere in sight.

Then Sam came staggering up to me from behind. 'Where've you been, you old dog?' His out-breaths were laboured, his mouth twisted into the usual grimacing leer and he was too close to me. 'I–I saw you go off with that pretty girl. What you done with her?'

I shrugged and slunk away from the bar; I'd been waylaid more than once, and his ramblings made my ears hurt.

They started playing 'Let's Go Round Again' and I thought about dancing. It would get rid of Sam and perhaps make things feel normal again, but I felt bad. I thought I ought to at least look for her. I downed my drink in one—well, perhaps two—then rushed through a good search of the room.

'Hell fire!' Sam slurred and shook his head at me, making the hair around his ears and neck flare out like tassels on a lampshade. 'Get on!'

No Ginny. My hands were killing me where friction from the pole had burned them. I waited to see if she'd come out of the ladies', then retraced our steps outside again, right back up the village to the church. I started wondering whether she'd even come back to the Joiners with me at all. By the time I got as far as the phone box I was imagining what I'd say to the ambulance and police. What did they do when you failed to report an accident? When I crossed the road to the green I'd almost totally lost it and half-expected to find her body at the bottom of the flagpole.

But the flagpole was just the flagpole. There was nothing to see, no Ginny on the ground or in the porch. She was nowhere.

I went back to the pub and stood outside the disco at the bottom of the back stairs, shaking my head and telling myself I'd done nothing wrong. Sam came outside and looked at me; my hair was plastered to my head and I was dripping.

'You're not right, you,' he said, his voice thick. 'Hi Ho Silver Lining' was blasting out behind him; time to go.

It shook me up, I'll admit that. I was glad to be shot of her right enough, but every time I passed that flagpole on the way to work and back, I brooded on what *could* have happened, and that drove me as mad as not knowing where she'd gone and if she was okay. Sometimes I went round by Wennington to avoid it. Even then I didn't feel as if I'd shaken her off properly. It was like I had a piece of grit in my eye.

I ended up moving to Glasgow. I was interviewed, worked my notice, packed up and was gone within the month. My mum was upset, but it did me good. I spread my wings, got out of my comfort zone—and Burton's as comfortable a zone as you're likely to find. I just wanted to bury myself in a crowd, and I can put up with a bit of concrete and traffic.

So my claim to fame is this: one night I was watching the telly and a famous ballerina was being interviewed on *The One Show*. It was Ginny. I might even have heard of her before then if I ever took notice of such things. That explains her shinnying up that flagpole—a pole dancer before her time. Her face was still long and thin, her hair still auburn but the curls were smoothed up into a typical ballerina topknot and there were some lines around her eyes. Her voice was unrecognisable. Smooth and musical and transatlantic.

I don't tell people about the night we met; I just say I once danced with Ginny Benjamin and took her for a walk in the dark.

56

River Lune
Mary Sylvia Winter

I do not know much about rivers
but it seems to me that this river undergoes a
personality change
just about here at the base of Castle Hill.
Higher up the valley
it seems more lighthearted.
You can stand on the grassy bank
and cast your wishes into the water,
watch them drift away with the current,
bobbing gently towards fulfilment.

But here in town,
where the river becomes tidal,
We have always known
that water rises and banks need fortifying.
we have always lived with the stench.

We still see the shadow
cast upon the ripples
of bodies dancing on the ends of ropes
just up the hill at the castle.
We still hear echoes from the quay
of the oars of the slaving ships
that made us rich.
Don't cast your wishes here, the river warned us;
don't conjure with me.
But we've never listened.
The water swells with our wishes
for wealth, vengeance, conquest
always at somebody else's expense.
Maybe that is why the river seems implacable.
Maybe the murkiness, the oiliness, the slickness,
the sudden rising,
the mercilessness of this water
is nothing but our own reflection.

Wreaths

Clare Weze Easterby

My grandfather made Christmas wreaths. In summer, we would collect sphagnum moss on the moors, and from September to mid-December he would be frantically busy, wire frames to be made, holly to be collected. Two thousand wreaths for one shop, six hundred for another—thousands of wreaths in total. I didn't often go with him when he made his deliveries, but sometimes he needed me.

This day was bright but cold. There had been a hard frost and we set out after breakfast into a veil of freezing fog, which cleared soon after we reached the main road. The Austin Allegro was stacked to the ceiling with wreaths, as was the trailer behind it.

Granny tried to tangle us up in her goodbye chatter: 'Are you sure you're going to Lancaster and Morecambe first? I'd have gone via Carnforth. You've got three drops there, haven't you?' She was trying out a new hairstyle involving a complicated chignon, and white wisps were already unravelling onto her shirt collar. 'Then up to Silverdale and finish off in Lancaster so it's more of a round trip. You want nothing having to double back on yourselves, and....' But Grandad just put his eyebrows into the arched shape he used for listening. He cupped his smooth-shaven chin in one hand and nodded until she had finished, and I knew we'd do it his way.

She called to me as we pulled away, 'Smile, sweetheart! Smile!'

Silverdale was a good place to end up. The coastline was magical in winter, and I liked to look across the bay. It was silvery, like the name. Granny's endless chatter seemed to reverberate for miles; I think we'd reached Claughton before either of us spoke again.

Christmas music was playing in the first shop. Bing and David Bowie bar-rap-ap-bam-bammed, and the shopkeeper said, 'Now Bill,' to Grandad.

'How do, Stan.'

'Tha's gitten a young helper today.'

'Aye. I'm a bit puffed at present,' Grandad put a hand to his chest and smiled. 'But that's Farmer's Lung for you.'

Most of the time I tried not to think about Grandad's emphysema. His chest had been barrel-shaped for as long as I could remember. It had forced him into early retirement from farming, hence the wreath-making business and other enterprises. I couldn't imagine him doing farm work now. He was too tidy, too ready to wear suit jackets and ties, and I'd never known him to smell of anything other than Silvikrin hair lotion and pipe tobacco.

'And what age have you gitten to now, young lady?'

'I'm twelve,' I said. I remembered to smile.

'Nay! Already?' The shopkeeper widened his eyes at Grandad. 'Nay, Bill. Growing up.'

'Aye,' said Grandad. They both stared at me with sad smiles and shook their heads.

'I'll start unloading,' I said, and escaped to the car. There was a warehouse at the back of the shop, and that's where I took the first box of wreaths. Grandad had reversed our car and trailer up to a gateway at the side of the building, so the distance to walk was minimal, but inside, the warehouse was silent. The field opposite still had thick patches of frost on it, like sprinklings of grey-white icing sugar. Some crows in the distant trees cawed at each other with broken, irritated voices. The sky was streaked with pink.

The old man startled me. He must have appeared while I was watching the field and listening to the crows. 'Mind you,' he said, as if he'd been talking to me a moment ago. So I was confused. I stood and stared.

'Mind you, you wouldn't think it was Christmas with all this hot weather,' he said. I looked at the frost out in the field, then back to the coarse black hairs sprouting from his ears. *Probably someone's grandad, but a thousand miles from my own.* My jacket flopped forward and caught on the wreaths as I put them down, springing out some moss.

'Never anywhere to stash a sheep or a pig. Where do you keep yours?' His large nostrils looked damp and red as if they might have glistened with moisture just moments ago and could start running again any second.

'I haven't got any, and I'm busy doing these,' I said, and started to transfer the wreaths to a row of empty shelves. His eyes seemed to look through me and slightly to the side, making me want to turn and see what was behind me. He edged closer, like a dog that wanted a stroke. I took a step back, but he was now so close that I could smell him. Something sweet, like cake... something musty... something bodily... Rank because it was so personal rather than because he was unwashed.

'I've got a lovely litter of piglets. Come into the back here and I'll show you.' He pointed to a little recess next to the door. It was an empty space, a shadowy place. I realised then what Granny meant when she'd said, 'Even if you know them... *especially* if you know them.' Because I didn't know this man but we'd just been talking, so I was trapped in a net of embarrassment—my own net as much as his.

'You're on the skinny side, aren't you dear?' he said as I picked up the empty box. 'Not that I mind. You are what you are, that's what I always say. I once knew a man who looked like a walking skeleton. He'd have frightened you.'

There was a pause, which seems crazy to me now. Why didn't I run?

'Well, come on,' he said, looking from me to the recess. The flaps of skin hanging between his chin and his neck wobbled as he moved his head.

'My grandad's only through there,' I said at last, bold and

cross.

'Ah, but where is through there? It's another world, a world away... unreachable.'

Fear hit me in the belly first, then the legs. They shook but didn't buckle. To drop the box and run, to make one sharp movement might unleash a movement of his. He might be old, but he was bigger than me, and he didn't look puny.

'Okay then,' I said in a high voice. 'I'll just ask.'

I ran away, breath, vocal chords and chest prepared to scream at the first touch. None came. When I got back to Grandad, I didn't tell him. I couldn't put worry onto that face. 'Will you come with me for the rest?' I said.

There was no sign of the man when we got back. No visible trace, as if there had never been anyone else there at all, but the smell of him was on me, up my nose, not in the air. I used all my senses to feel for him, for where he'd been, but all I gleaned from the air in the shed was that static, everything-waiting-for-Christmas mood.

It only took three more trips to complete that delivery with two of us unloading. Adrenaline made me move fast.

'Not so much sweat,' said Grandad. 'We've got all day.' He stopped to poke a wayward berry sprig down into its cross-shaped wreath and I saw his workshop with its radio and gas heater and the stacks of wire frames, moss packed and tied, holly sprigs waiting—all the stages of our little industry. My mind has done this many times since—focused on a series of details to drown out an unpleasant sight or thought—but I've never again seen anything as vivid as those wreaths and their construction.

'Thanking you,' Grandad said to Stan as we left, and I'm sure my face was normal, but the stranger's musty-sweet furniture polish smell harried my nostrils all through the Morecambe and Carnforth deliveries. By Silverdale, I had stopped feeling sick and shaky, but when I looked out over the bay, it seemed grey and distinctly un-magical. I tried to focus on the horizon and think of faraway places, but it didn't work.

I caved in a little on the journey home.

'There was a funny old man in Mr. Wilson's warehouse,' I

said, inviting explanation, expecting Grandad to tell me it was just the shopkeeper's brother.

'Oh? What was he doing?'

'Just looking for something, probably,' I said cheerfully. I glanced at him. He wasn't frowning, but his features were poised on the edge of it and the Allegro juddered in fifth gear, needing to be driven faster.

The short winter day was almost over. The smell in my nostrils had become a taste in my mouth, but I was exhilarated, almost jubilant at the thought of getting home to Granny's chatter, and she didn't let me down.

She had made a chicken curry and gave us a breakdown of its ingredients, her slimness meaningless beneath the weight of the pots she hefted around.

'The piano teacher's parents have got an L-shaped living room with a dining table at one end, you know,' she said as we took our first mouthfuls. We donned our listening faces and looked at her without answering.

I didn't go to my room that evening. Instead, I dried the dishes without being asked.

'The Cairn sisters are going to a new dog show in Birmingham,' Granny said, but she looked at me and questions waited in the air. She stacked five rinsed plates one after the other in quick succession, then eyed me as I turned to cross the room and put things away. 'It's a long way for the dogs to travel.'

Granny's chatter was a firewall. I could see that now, and without it, the night would creep closer. I watched her quick, yellowed-gloved fingers slip over the dishes. All the fretting was in her fingers; there was none in her voice.

She went on. 'I did say, actually, I don't know if Miss Cairn really took it in. I don't think she knows how far Birmingham actually is.'

I let her details dribble all around me, chasing away everything she had seen and everything I knew.

First Silaging, First Day

--for Trevor, among others
Mary Sylvia Winter

Today,
rounding a bend in the road,
I saw on the slopes above Aughton
the first green-on-green stripes
of silo time.
And my heart leapt.

Now why was that?
Generations have passed
since my bloodlines flowed away from the soil
    (if they ever can).
My living does not depend
on the weight of grass from those fields
    (only my life).

And if you, sweating on your tractor,
were to stop beneath the window
    of my ivory study,
and hear me murmuring
about the resonance of the soil
and the eternal gladness of harvest,

you would probably roll your eyes,
thinking wryly,
as you let in the clutch,
that my heart had no business doing any leaping.

But my heart did leap.
It did, truly.

The Visitor
Clare Weze Easterby

Christopher crossed Main Street nimbly—he felt he'd moved like
the very devil—but he wasn't in time to avoid Mrs. Morrison.
*Still fussing about bees eating into the wood of her window
frames*, he thought. *Still intent on trapping me.*

'Oh, *now* then, thank goodness. I want to know what to treat
it with and you'll know the answer. I'm determined not to harm
them—we need bees, especially now—but it's getting to the point
where—'

Christopher held both hands up in the air between them.
'Sorry, I have my cottage to see to. It's changeover day.'

'Oh yes, it's Saturday. I know it's busy for you but—'

'Sorry! Need to get there before the cleaner.'

Teaspoons were on his mind. Last week's visitors managed
to get the total down to two. *Two! What do they do with them?
And why?* He approached the cottage with caution, but all was
clear. No car in the drive, no last-minute suitcase fumblers. He let
himself in and breathed in burnt toast.

By the time he'd opened every window and door, Chloe arrived.

'Can you still smell it?' he asked her. 'Breakfast. Every
Saturday's the same! Haven't people heard of fresh air?'

'Hi, Mr. Neville.' Chloe put the clean linen on the table and
pulled the cleaning trug out from under the sink.

The visitors' book wasn't in its usual place on the dining
table; not a good sign. Christopher tracked it down to the kitchen

71

windowsill—a ridiculous place—and opened it with the usual dread.

'"Everything beautifully clean, marvellous views, cosy, appreciated homely touches"—Ah, here we are. I thought it was too good to be true—"apart from the cooker. You need a degree to operate it. What's wrong with a good old-fashioned on/off switch?"' He snapped the book shut. 'What am I supposed to do about that? Am I a cooker *manufacturer*? What's the matter with these people?'

Chloe made a non-committal noise and carried on wiping the oven.

'And it's a brand new appliance! Remember last week? A complaint about the dishwasher—"it failed to empty properly on the heavy soil programme." They don't even need a dishwasher—it's an *extra*, for God's sake!'

Chloe closed the oven door and straightened her back. 'But they've written nice things too, haven't they?'

'That's not the point. That's not what new visitors notice when they read the book.'

'I concentrate on the nice things.' Chloe moved to the fridge and Christopher started inspecting the cupboards. He missed Mrs. Major. Chloe was quite thorough for a young one, and very open to the idea that one had to obliterate all signs of human habitation on changeovers, but Mrs. Major had an unfathomable system whereby rooms were swept through without a moment's standing still. She would have the beds stripped and the sheets tumbling round the washer while the first few rooms were cleaned, then out and on the line and only taken home for ironing. Chloe never seemed to get them on the line. She brought them back the next week clean and smooth, but without that line-dried freshness.

He returned his visitors' book to its rightful place on the dining table, but couldn't resist opening the ruined pages again:

I saw a mouse! This property is a HEALTH HAZARD.

The kitchen tiles are too hard for my baby.

72

Rain again. This is a useless part of the world if you want to go outside.

Hadn't expected to be quite so close to the road. "Quiet location" it is not.

He closed the book and returned to his cupboards.

'Oh for heaven's sake, look at this!'

Chloe stopped wiping and turned round, startled.

'A pan! A dirty pan! Someone has put a *dirty* pan back amongst the *clean*. Could you even believe anybody would be so imbecilic?'

Chloe stepped towards him, holding her hands out for the pan. 'I'll sort it out; don't worry.'

'No, the whole lot will have to be inspected now.'

'I'll see to it. Don't—'

'You can't be expected to do this kind of thing every week on top of the basic cleaning, Chloe. What sort of people put things back dirty? Do they do it in their own homes?'

There was a knock at the door. Christopher opened it to find an elderly gentleman clutching a rucksack.

'Three p.m.,' Christopher said, turning the dirty pan over in his hands. 'Not before, ever—the cottage isn't ready, you see. Changeovers take time.'

This was a short-notice phone booking, he remembers. The client had had a very shaky voice. The gentleman didn't appear to understand and continued to wait on the doorstep. He looked incredibly old and frail and seemed to have travelled in his slippers.

'If you'd be kind enough to wait in your car, Mr... Keane?' Christopher gazed at the car-less drive.

'I've come by bus.'

'Oh. Right. Well, if you wouldn't mind just taking a seat,' Christopher stepped past him onto the patio and pulled out a garden chair. 'We'll be as fast as possible.'

'Very good.' Slowly and carefully, the gentleman sat down. He smoothed a hand over brown corduroy trousers. 'By gum, the

73

lilac's grown!'

'The lilac? You've stayed here before?'

'This was our first house.'

First house? What on earth is he talking about? 'You used to live here? Oh. I see. And will your wife be joining you?'

'Oh yes. I'm expecting her any time... yes.' He looked as content as anyone Christopher had ever seen.

Back inside the cottage, Christopher rushed through the rest of the cleaning, avoiding the rooms Chloe was working on. His polishing, although rusty (why have a dog and bark yourself?) was second to none, and ten minutes on the coffee table produced a mirror-like shine. He took a dry duster and rubbed again, slowly now, wondering about the elderly man alone in his garden.

Chloe brought Mr. Keane in when everything was finished. 'Bye then. See you next week.' She left him in the kitchen. Only one rucksack, thought Christopher. The wife must be bringing the rest.

'Right. The date will come up, if you'd like to check it?' He held his videophone under the old man's nose. Mr. Keane glanced at it without a shred of understanding, but Christopher pressed on anyway. 'Okay. Cupboards.' He pulled them open one by one, filmed their contents then slid them shut. 'Microwave. It's virtually brand new and very easy to operate. Kettle.'

'Champion. Annie's never been struck on microwaves, but I like to warm a cup of tea!'

This guest didn't seem to notice or mind him filming. Usually they looked at him as if he were an executioner.

'I mended a gap in the far meadow on the morning of our wedding,' Mr. Keane said. 'I had to. I had cows arriving ten days later.'

'Ah. You were a farmer?'

'Aye.'

Christopher sometimes forgot the place was once a farm. Everything was divided so neatly, the converted outbuildings appeared settled in their landscaping and the fields at the back were just some farmer's fields. 'Okay, that's the kitchen done. We'll move on to the sitting room.' Christopher filmed every nook

74

and cranny and the old man followed him from room to room, reminiscing. Sometimes Christopher tuned into it.

'I was really red in the face and I stuttered one or twice, but I did it, I asked her out. Nothing would have stopped me. I think she could see that in my face.'

Christopher blinked. 'I'm sorry?'

'Annie, I asked her to the races.'

'Oh... oh I see, sorry.' Things seemed to have slipped backwards from the wedding day.

'Have you always been a bachelor?'

Christopher stopped filming and blinked again. He couldn't remember saying *what* he was... 'Yes. Just never bothered with any of that.' He closed his phone and picked up his briefcase. 'Right! Have a lovely stay. Don't hesitate to contact me, etc. etc., as I'm just round the corner. Directions are in the guest file, which lives here,' he laid a hand flat on a file on top of a chest of drawers in the sitting room, 'and only here. Bye for now.'

Christopher left it two days, but Mr. Keane niggled at the corners of his mind. He looked like the perfect guest—acquiescent, appreciative—but Christopher mistrusted perfection. And the old man was so, well... *old*. Then he remembered the cooker instructions; it couldn't hurt to go over them with him again. He found Mr. Keane in the garden, sitting in the sun wearing a straw trilby.

'Everything satisfactory? I just wanted to make sure you were fine with the cooker. Seems to present some people with problems.'

Inside, the kitchen was pin-neat, as if no food had been prepared at all. There was a smell of Silvikrin in the air. Christopher went through the cooker instructions and the old man listened patiently. There was no other sound anywhere.

'Your wife—has she been held up?'

'That's right. Held up. I expect she'll be arriving any time now.' Mr. Keane shuffled along, then reached for a cup next to the kettle. 'Oh, I found this in the bottom of the wardrobe.' He grinned. 'A kiddie must have left it. Perhaps you could dry it out

75

and send it on.'

Christopher peered into the cup. A gloopy green embryonic shape curled up at the bottom of it. 'Good grief! I do apologise, Sir. I'll go up and check if there's a mess to mop up.'

'No mess. It's all fine. The whole house is just champion, Annie will be suited to bits at how you've looked after it.'

'I can't imagine how Chloe missed it.'

Chloe's cottage was a few doors away from the Methodist church, but Christopher marched straight round there in under two minutes.

'This was in the wardrobe of the master bedroom.' He held out the embryo, still in its cup. 'And it just shows, Chloe, as I keep impressing on you, that you really do *have* to go over every inch of the house *every* single week.'

Chloe stared down into the cup, then took it from his hands. 'Oh... it's an alien.'

'I'm sorry?'

'An alien. The kids have them sometimes. They come in eggs and they're supposed to grow if you keep them in water. I always wondered if that was really true.' She fished inside the cup and pulled out the green gloop.

'Disgusting item! To have left it in a wardrobe of all places!'

'Mmm... dead squishy. That's why the kids love them.'

'It doesn't belong to one of *your* children does it, Chloe?'

'Oh no, no. Mine haven't been anywhere near.' Her children were around in the rooms behind her; he could neither see nor hear them, but they were there. Always, when he walked away from Chloe's house, he had the feeling that people were pulling faces behind his back.

'Good. Well if you just bear in mind what I've said for the future. It's just as well it happened this week, as this chap doesn't seem to mind much at all. Strange chap. Seems to live on nothing. No sign of mess in the house.'

'Must be an old soldier.'

'I beg your pardon?'

'They're known for being able to look after themselves,

76

keep everything spick and span.'

'Oh. No, I believe he was a farmer. With no wife. As yet.'

Ignoring Chloe's questioning look, he went home and got on with the rest of his day's tasks. *No wife.... Something wrong there, but not my problem. As long as the house is left in good condition, the man can have ten wives or none.*

Nevertheless, Christopher found himself back with Mr. Keane again that very afternoon. He was offered a coffee and accepted it, which was unheard of—he always kept holiday cottagers at a respectable distance—but he sat in the cottage garden. Mr. Keane rattled on from time to time, and Christopher even listened to half of it. He found himself in an unusual, musing kind of mood. Somehow, the song 'I'll Be Seeing You' began to chime away in his mind... *in all the old familiar places.* It was saddening, and after half an hour or so he turned his attention to more pressing matters: the visitor's book. Mr. Keane was a good listener.

'They're incompetents and ignorami, the people who write these comments,' Christopher stroked the fake leather binding and traced the gold lettering of the word *Visitors'*.

'Well, people do like to moan. Makes them feel better.'

'Yes. Like the idiots in the firm I used to work for. The Peter Principle indeed!'

'Now then, I made my living in cows and sheep, so I'm not well up on these new phrases.'

'The Peter Principle states that people tend to rise to their level of incompetence, so useless shop floor workers become useless managers and so on till they reach the very top. It's amazing the things people throw at you when your back's against the wall.'

Mr. Keane nodded. 'Aye, that's likely.' He stared into the heart of the lilac tree.

'Spurious accusations dreamt up by total nonentities. Still, it enabled me to buy this place.'

Mr. Keane looked puzzled.

'Golden handshake.'

'Oh... ah... well, that's champion then.'

Christopher stretched out his fingers until the knuckles cracked. 'Left them to it. Let them stew in their own juice.'

'That's the spirit. Will you have a slice of plain cake?' He said it as if Christopher would be doing him a favour by accepting. *Plain cake.* He hadn't heard it called that for quite some time.

'Thank you, yes.'

Grey clouds rolled across from the fell and the sun disappeared. Christopher continued to talk through to the kitchen while Mr. Keane rustled inside. 'We'd come to Newbiggin for holidays when I was a child. Used to ramble in the fields, go fishing in the streams. Never forgotten it.'

'Ah.' Mr. Keane came back with cake on two plates and sat down again, slowly. 'I'll have to rack my brains and see if I remember you. It was popular with kiddies was our Dutch Barn pasture.'

A car turned into the drive. Christopher rose to his feet, heart beating fast. 'What on Earth?' Then he calmed down. It was probably the missing wife. Two people got out, one wearing a moss green nurse's uniform. The other, a man about a decade younger than Christopher, looked flushed and anxious. Both of them looked at Mr. Keane, then walked towards Mr. Keane, and Christopher's neck muscles began to tense.

Mr. Keane lifted his eyebrows and beamed. 'Mark!'

'Dad.' The man's eyes met Christopher's. He shook his head. 'Dad,' he said again, and he bent and took hold of both Mr. Keane's hands.

Christopher shifted, glancing between them.

'I'm really sorry—you must be the owner. We've been looking for Dad all over the place. He's an escapee I'm afraid— The Beeches Retirement Home, all the way from Nottingham. Dad,' he shook Mr. Keane's hands gently. 'You didn't let anyone know you were coming here. People have been very worried.'

Mr. Keane smiled broadly, still looking serene, still sitting. 'Haven't the conifers grown! Just look at the size of them!'

Christopher looked. Ridiculous things, like towering sentinels. He shook his head, feeling the prickle of sweat around

78

his hairline. 'But I don't understand—'

Mr. Keane still squeezed his son's hands. 'Annie loves conifers. They were her idea really. I was worried about them taking the place over, but they haven't done too bad, have they?'

'No, Dad. Come on, let's get your stuff.'

'I'll see to all that.' The carer put an arm around Mr. Keane's shoulder and lifted his hand lightly. 'Come on, Mr. Keane, let's get going. We've got a long journey and we need you to be bright and breezy when we get back because your daughter's coming to see you. *That's* right.'

Christopher listened to the endless-rivers-of-patience in her voice. 'I had no idea—'

The carer led Mr. Keane into the house and the son turned to Christopher. 'Sorry to have inconvenienced you.'

'Well, it's been no trouble... none at all... it's just that I didn't realise—'

'He doesn't know why he's in The Beeches any more, you see, or that our mother's dead. It seemed cruel to keep telling him that over and over, every week, so we thought it best if he believed what he liked.'

'He's seems... perfectly lucid... perfectly capable.' Christopher glanced at the kitchen window. 'Everything is spotless.' The kitchen worktops, untouched. *What can he have been living on? Cake?*

'My sister blames herself. She showed him your cottage in the agency brochure, to prove that it really has gone out of the family. Because he was so fixated, you see. We just couldn't get him off the topic at all. And then he must have kept the blasted thing because she couldn't find it again to phone you, so I just thought we'd drive on up here anyway. It was a good bet.'

Christopher nodded.

Within five minutes it was all over and they were leading Mr. Keane away, one on either side of him. Afterwards, Christopher stood in the empty kitchen with the back door still open. It started raining, light but steady, tiny sounds bouncing off the leaves and gravel like a symphony, shivering through Mr. Keane's lilac.

79

Zosia
Melissa Bailey

I met Dodge in the pub where I work.

He was a bit scruffy. Not really the type of customer they like here. He was a hangover from the pub in the old days before Mr Steinman bought it, converted it and changed the name from The Three Horseshoes to The Sun Inn. Really it's more of a restaurant now.

People come from the city for a nice drive out to the Dales and the pub is on the outskirts of the village, sign painted olive green as if we're some National Trust property. We serve meals like Harissa Chicken in a soured cream crust and kiwi lime tart. People park their cars and sink into the big leather sofas and say to each other 'Wouldn't it be nice to live in the Lune Valley?' as they flick through a copy of Lancashire Life. But then they see the price of the houses...

So Dodge didn't really fit with his scruffy clothes but I liked him. I could see he was good looking under all that grime. Bits of his body poked through the torn trousers and open necked shirts. I don't think his name was really that but we all called him 'Dodge' after the bus he lived in.

I couldn't understand what an intelligent guy like that was doing living rough.

I was always trying to encourage him to make more of himself. He's good with his hands. One evening a few weeks before Christmas the electricity crashed and it was chaos in the kitchen. We were expecting a big party in from the local doctor's. Twenty of them – receptionists and nurses and some doctors for their Christmas three course meal. We tried the trip switch but it wasn't anything as simple as that. Dodge offered to help...
Turned out that the fan in the kitchen was clogged up with grease and some wires were burnt through but Dodge managed to reconnect the wires and sort it all out. Even after that, the manager would stare him out if he stayed after seven when the diners arrived.

He'd turn up the minute we opened, drink two or three steady pints, always the cheapest ale, and then he'd leave. He made me laugh, which is more than I can say for most of the people who come in. They are so fussy.

One night he came in late. The place usually shuts after the diners leave at ten and I could see that he was drunk. The manager wasn't amused. But it had been hard work, I'd got a few orders muddled up. I know my English seems good but I don't always understand people's accents. It was quietening down and I was grateful for a friendly face.

82

I could feel the way he was looking at me – you know – his eyes skimming my backside when I turned round to the till. But he was kind of cute so I was enjoying it. I was intrigued by his bus – he was always talking about it and working on it – and he invited me back to see it. So after I cleaned up the bar and wiped down the floor I went out to see the bus.

It was in a bit of state. It reminded me of my Grandad's hut back in Poland where he used to go to hide from my Grandma – it smelt of onions and bulbs lifted for the winter and there was faded nylon fabric on the seats.

There was a little burner converted from a gas canister and he drove me up a steep hill onto the fells then made us a cup of tea. We sat in the front and looked out at the stars. It was mid-December and the time of year when the Perseids meteor showers can be seen and you know what it's like, once you've seen one shooting star you just can't help waiting for the next, so we sat there for a couple of hours – 'Did you see that one? Wow – look at that' and he told me his dreams about driving around the world and living outside the system and being really free… I tell him my dreams of running my own business and driving round in a Merc convertible and having a nice house which I own...

His ideas seem so daft. I mean, there he was living in this beautiful Lune Valley village where he'd grown up with his parents and he was dossing in an old bus... I know his parents – they come into the pub once in a while. They seem nice people. They have a lovely cottage. But they'd all fallen out, for some reason I never did find out.

Listen, I'm ambitious and most of my friends are too. We've seen how tough life can be and here he was throwing everything on some dream of a bus… anyway then we shared a bottle of beer – he didn't have much else there but tea and beer – and then after two in the morning he drove me back down to the village.

I didn't see him over Christmas and New Year. Not sure where he disappeared to and we were rushed off our feet in the pub. I wasn't that concerned but I did wonder. Apparently he did sometimes disappear – went off on a 'bender' – but when he walked back in it was as if nothing had happened. I tried to put him out of my mind. I convinced myself he was just a waster and would do me no good at all.

I'm studying business and languages at the University and after Christmas I was asked out by the tutor of my flatmate. I'd met him a few times at a quiz in the student's bar. A lot of guys ask me out and usually I say no straight away unless I'm really keen, it avoids all kinds of complications. But I'd never been asked out by a lecturer before and anyway he wasn't *my* lecturer, so I thought it would be alright.

Andrew drove me to the Inn at Whitewell – I'd heard about it but never been there. It's quite famous round here. The wine was expensive and we ate oysters and then Bowland lamb in Madeira. We talked a bit about Poland. I was feeling homesick; my mother had been ill and I hadn't been back for Christmas. Andrew said he liked Poland – he'd been to some conference there – and he even knew a few words and treated me nice and helped me into my coat and opened the car door and paid for everything and on the way back home he stopped the car, kissed me on the lips and told me he'd like to see me again. He was a gentleman and I thought, well at least he treats me well and pays for me, I could do worse.

But that night I slept with Dodge for the first time.

He'd stayed late in the pub. Trev, who was in charge that night and knows Dodge from way back, shut up the bar and we carried on drinking. I was on the vodka, knocking back the snake bites and Dodge and I got into a long conversation about some book he'd been reading on Buddhism and then I went back to the bus to discuss some more and he drove me up to the fells so we could see the sun rise. Lucky the burner was still going and the van was lovely and warm as it was freezing outside.

Actually he was a bit rough as a lover. Almost angry. As if he couldn't wait to get me undressed and then it was over so quickly. As if he despised himself for wanting me or even for having any desire at all. That's Buddhism for you.

When I woke up he was still sleeping. I didn't know where I was – up on the bloody moor somewhere. I got out of the bus and started walking.… But there was a whipping wind and I could only see dirty sheep and moorland and I was in my work skirt and white blouse and a thin jacket so I went back to the bus and tried to wake him. He was in such a foul mood and refused to take me back to the village. I was pretty angry I can tell you.

I created a fuss so reluctantly he drove me back and I thought – ok, never again, Zosia. Too much vodka and that's what happens and anyway he was lousy in bed.

Later that week Andrew phoned. I'd given him my number. He asked what I was doing at the weekend. Working, I said, except for Sunday night. So on the Sunday night he bought me dinner, at a little Italian place in town and when he suggested going back to his flat after dinner I said yes, and he was the opposite of Dodge – he was gentle and grateful and not in bad shape for a man of his age – I found out he was 45 that evening.

I found out quite a lot of other things in the Scalini restaurant as we ate our tortellini. His wife had left him, taking the two teenage daughters with her. I thought at one stage he might cry as he was telling me about his daughters, who he now only saw once a week. He was renting a nice flat in a quiet area of the city. Sleek black furniture. Very tidy. Again I thought, Zosia, you can do worse than this. Good salary. Not bad looking. Nice car for a lecturer. A BMW. Bit bonkers about his ex-wife but apart from that... He put on some music – it was old 60s and 70s stuff – Pink Floyd, Kraftwerk – but I could cope with that. He was an IT specialist. Maybe he could help me get my translation business set up online. There were possibilities here. And like I said, he wasn't bad in bed either. Knew that a woman needs a little time to relax. And he was very grateful.

So there I am. Settling quite nicely into a routine with Andrew. We'd see each other once in the week and then on a Sunday I'd go back to his flat. And for a couple of months I don't see much of Dodge. But then he walks back into the bar one day, full of swagger. He's been working as a mechanic in Morecambe and he's got money in his pocket. There's a Polish proverb, 'Money is a powerful aphrodisiac. But flowers work almost as well.' At the time I'm looking for a new car as my VW needs work and I don't think it's worth the expense. Dodge tells me about this mate who's selling a Merc convertible. He knows it's the car I've always dreamed about. A couple of phone calls later and Dodge's arranged for us to take a trip to Barrow and see this car.

Dodge says this chap outside Barrow owes him a favour and I think Dodge owes me one so… It's a silver convertible, nice looking car, not new but not old, and Dodge thinks it kosher and we take it out for a drive and it feels great. After a bit of persuading on the phone, my Dad agrees to go halves and so I spend my savings on the car. Dad's keen on Mercs and there aren't many convertibles in Poland so he could sell it on when I go home.

My family haven't always been in the motor trade and they haven't always been rich. They were big landowners in the old days before the war. But then the communists come along and took all their land. They give the family back a few fields but my Dad's elder brother drank it away.

So we were always on the move and always poor. My Dad had no skills and his family were not popular. He found work where he could, in factories or on the land. I remember nothing happy or settled about that time. We were always moving from one grey apartment to another. But when the communists were kicked out, my Dad and his other brother start importing cars from Germany – old Mercedes and Audis – and soon they are making a profit and building up the family fortune again.

My Dad is thinking of expanding to Britain, especially now the pound's so weak, one of the reasons I'm here I guess. I've already got a first class degree in Poland but an English degree is worth more.

On the way back from Barrow – I was driving the Merc and Dodge was rattling along behind in the VW – we saw a sign for Walney Island. I'd never been there and it sounded kinda cute. I pulled over and what I like about Dodge is that he's up for adventure so off we went to Walney. Well cute it wasn't – except for the gnomes in the caravan park – it was windswept and bleak. We got a pack of Grolsch and climbed the dunes. There was no

86

one else around. Before I know it, Dodge's on top of me and it wasn't so bad this time. There's a nudist beach at the north end of the island and it was sunny enough for us to take off our clothes and lie naked in the dunes drinking beer, which was something I'd never dream of doing with anyone else but with Dodge it seemed quite natural.

Sometimes I stand in front of the bathroom mirror. I share a flat with this Greek student Maria – the one who introduced me to Andrew – and we've got a long mirror in the bathroom. I stand there and think – what do men see in this body? Or would any woman's body do? I take care of myself; I swim at the uni pool twice a week. I like to get there early and be the first to break into the water with no one around to watch me, the water rippling over my head. I like my thighs and my ankles. If I stand with one hip jutted forwards there's a curvy line from my shoulders to my feet and I can see my proportions are nicely balanced. I like it when the brown hairs on my arm turn gold in the summer and the streaks in my hair turn more blonde. I'm pretty happy with the way I look now even if it wasn't always so…

Andrew always says nice things to me – he appreciates me – runs his hands over me like I'm a fine horse or… that doesn't sound so good but he was brought up with horses, his mother is one of those horsey women and I can tell he likes fine things in life like good wines and Kalamata olives and Reblochon cheese…

But with Dodge it's always a little bit crazy. Like we're out on the edge, sails taut in the wind. He takes me walking on the moors and laughs when I protest about the mud and the bogs and the smelly sheep. One lunchtime he came into the pub and told me he'd found something to show me. I was supposed to be back in town for an afternoon lecture. I'd promised myself I would ignore Dodge and concentrate on Andrew… but I thought a walk won't hurt. It was a damp but mild day. He likes it when I drive him fast in the Merc with the hood down. We cruised the country lanes and then he directed me to a wood in a steep valley. It was dripping wet and the twigs cracked as we walked – the trees stained with moss and everything grey and green and brown. We

87

picked our way over bracken and brambles and there in a steep dell – with no paths leading to it or away from it – was a ruined stone building. We climbed down and went inside.

It had no roof and trees were growing out of it. What is it? A chapel? A barn? A cottage? Dodge didn't seem to know. I could feel myself fall a little in love with him then. Even though I'd promised myself I'd brush him off. I touched the clints and grykes of his face. The scar above his eyebrow where he'd been in a fight. I could see him for what he was – slightly crazy, his body ravaged by drink and drugs and the endless rollups; untrustworthy, unreliable, mad for sex in the open air. I knew I should close myself against him but why be cautious when you've only got one life?

We walked back, losing our way several times. It must have been spring cos I was running my fingers along the branches, touching the buds, brown with red tips, and a weak sun was filtering through the branches.

I was saying I 'should' get back and Dodge said 'bollocks' to the 'shoulds' in life.

Soon after that the car broke down and then there was always some problem or other with it – I'm afraid I paid too much for that old wreck. But Dodge would be under that bonnet for hours and he'd come into the bar covered in grease and the manager would be annoyed.

So he'd wait till I was free and he'd take me out for a drive to prove the car was running just fine again. And he'd show me something new. One day later that spring we went searching for purple flowering orchids and found several in a patch of sun deep in the woods. He taught me how to recognise the plaintive call of the curlew; the 'getbackgetbackgetback' of the grouse up on the moor, and in the summer we spent hours parked up beyond the cattlegrid, watching the acrobatic lapwings roll and dive above the fields, crying 'pee-wit, wit, wit-eeze, wit'.

Then in the autumn I heard that Dodge had been arrested.

I never knew what happened. He was one of those people who come into your life and they leave a mark; he stirred the air like winter rain then he was gone. He never made any promises about staying in touch or being faithful.

I still think of him often. I wonder whether he's in prison. But I don't know who to ask and I can't afford to get caught up in anything which might affect my immigration status. I'm hoping that I get naturalised, you see. Another year and then I can go for the test. After that I'd like to set up my business here. I've had enough of bar work. But there's not much other work in the valley.

Andrew has been hinting that we might buy a house. He says he doesn't ever want to get married again but he's not averse to living with me. He wants me to get rid of the Merc and has promised me a new car for Christmas. Without Dodge to maintain it, I might as well scrap the car, the bills are getting so bad. There's a sweet cottage on the main street with roses in the front garden. I keep looking at it and imagining what it might be like to live there... At night when I can't sleep I calm myself down by imagining houses which one day might be mine. I can waste hours looking at houses on Rightmove... I dream one day I could make a permanent life here in the village... build up my business and have enough money to buy and decorate a beautiful house like the ones I see in the magazines I tidy up at the end of the day. I know they won't ever accept a foreigner like me properly but I dream that my children could be safe here. That they could live in a fine house with bulbs which flower each spring in the garden and an Aga and a huge fridge and they will never know what it is to do without.

90

Dodge
Melissa Bailey

Why have I never been a house person? Houses do me head in. I was always building dens as a kid and the dens got more complicated and heavy duty as I got older. I had this shed at the top of the garden where I spent all my time, winter and summer; it was ace and it had old car seats and a table in it and we hung out there. When I look back, it was all a natural progression to where I am now, living in this bus. Sometimes I don't go into a house for a month or two and then you notice how it makes you feel and I'm just totally uncomfortable in a house.

I'd sooner live in a tent; to me a house is a last resort. I moved into a caravan when me dad chucked me out and I parked it up the top for two winters, but I had no burner in there and you'd wake up with your hair frozen to the pillow and some nights you couldn't sleep at all you was so cold.

Then I thought it would be better to have a bus cos you can move around and I could go wherever I felt like it and park up. I saw this Dodge bus; they're really heavy duty, an old design that can't go wrong, built in '86 from a set of diagrams. For three months I parked it in the pub car park and put this burner and the bed in. But people hate this bus. You can see the smoke and bits hanging off it and people started complaining. And then some creep bought the pub and turned it into a fancy restaurant and I wasn't welcome though I still go in once in a while. When I feel like it.

Getting an MOT for this thing was a nightmare too.

I tried everywhere but no one would MOT it. Then just before Christmas one garage in Morecambe said they'd look at it. I was so pleased and so the night before I went to park it up on the fells by the cattlegrid, which is one of one of my most favourite places in the world. It's where I do all my thinking. When I was a kid I used to bike up there and when I got my first car we went up there and smoked dope for hours. It's the perfect chilled out place to park, sheltered behind some trees with a little stream at the back and views for miles. But you've got to be organised. There's no shops and only stream water to drink. At dawn the sky changes from black through all the colours to pink and white, still dark behind you, daylight ahead. If you sit there all day you can watch the sun move across the sky. I've seen shoals of birds from miles away, flying up the Lune, using the river as a map as they migrate, none of them taking shortcuts, all moving together distinct and silver against the sky.

But that night before Christmas it was pissing down and the rain must have blown underneath into the brakes and when I woke up in the morning the brakes had jammed. I was kicking it and screaming and I'd lost my last bit of patience. I had to push it down the hill with my shoulder to get it started nearly killing myself. I got it to Morecambe, and all morning I was working on it, trying to get it ready for the MOT, but then the brakes jammed again. So there it was, parked outside this scrapyard, not budging, I was so narked off I was going to scrap it. I got this cutting gear to slice it to bits, and this guy said, 'What you doing? And I said, 'I'm brassed off with it,' 'No no, don't scrap it, don't jack it in.' They asked me what I was doing for Christmas I told them I was going off to kip somewhere but they persuaded me to stay on the bus and got me some beers and food from Asda and cleared me a space in the compound and that was how I ended up living in the scrapyard.

The bus was boxed against a high concrete wall so no one could get in through the windows; along the back was an old Merc removals van which had been there nearly a year, stored for an insurance company, all melted after a fire and minging and mouldy and full of rats. Behind the Merc van was this frag machine. It was massive, ten times bigger than the bus, and this thing was firing up from six in the morning till six at night. These JCBs grabbed the cars and put them on this conveyor belt, then these cutters and rollers fragmented the lot – so steel came out one bit, copper out of another. It would shake the ground with its noise, and if a caravan had been going through, all the insulation came out of this huge chimney, showering down over everything as a fine black dust. You could feel it sharp on your throat. I can't describe how filthy it was: it could kill you, minging and full of shite and oil.

You couldn't see the bus at all cos there were two other vans parked along the other sides and to get in and out you had to squeeze past these cars and climb over their bonnets. So out the window there was no sky, just black concrete and a radio communications mast and scrap cars.

This guy who I was working for is the dog's bollocks – totally sound. He just takes you on board and all your problems, I'll never ever say a word against him. He's made his money by pure hard work and he could have got into real trouble for letting me live in that scrapyard. He gave me the keys to the yard and a load of batteries and he let me charge them in the brew room cos he knew if my batteries were flat I'd have no lights or radio at night. If you met this guy you'd think he was hard as nails but deep down he's the business.

But after a couple of months of living there it all got too much. I got involved with the wrong people. You've got a dodgy subject, second hand cars, and a dodgy place, a scrapyard, and you've got all the ingredients for the scum of the earth to congregate and I was the bottom of the pile. You could buy women, drugs, anything measured out in diamonds there. You can't just say, Oh I'm from a village, and I like looking at the trees and the river. You fight to survive in those places, you've had it if they see your weak points.

I was getting absolutely steaming every night. It's a weird experience when you're in a city you don't know and you go into a rough pub and half the pub know you and you don't know

93

them. They'd say, 'Aren't you that lad who lives in a bus who I bought an alternator from? Get him a pint.' Everyone's always in and out of scrapyards and you get to meet all sorts of people; and they think, he looks scally, living on a bus, working in scrapyard. I learned about every kind of lock and ignition, so I knew how to hot wire and people want you to nick cars for them, and I just got drawn into stuff.

I used to sleep fully clothed with an axe stuffed down one side of my pillow and a gun underneath and one night I got back bladdered from the pub and I was just about to turn in when I heard these voices outside. Not just one or two. I had nothing on the bus to nick but I did have the key to the yard and I thought that was what they were after. There were a lot of cars in the compound ready for sale. So I got my phone, and put in the number of the police station, and held my finger over the button and got my axe in the other hand, and kicked the bus door open and shouted 'Come on scum, don't be scared,' cos you've got to pretend you re absolutely vicious to get the advantage. And at that minute I realized it was the police. There were dozens of them and they'd blocked the road and cordoned off the yard and they had this massive Alsatian that was growling and snapping and I said, 'What are you lot doing? I was about to ring you.' They must have thought I had a load of people on board and was selling smack. They were tough with me and I was hard with them. But the moment they looked in the door they could see the score; the bus was just full of beer cans, they could see it was only a place for dossing.

After that I fixed up the Dodge and some nights I'd go and park down at the docks at Heysham for a change of scene. When everything shuts up on the industrial estate, the truck drivers arrive, waiting for the ferries. It gets really busy after twelve or one, ferries and trucks coming and going, pulling up, unloading. It goes from daylight to orangelight, there's no such thing as dark there, time is meaningless to the truckers cos they drive all over the world, day and night. Some nights it's chock a block with trucks, they are nose to nose, and I used to back up and park there, go and get a Chinese, visit the pubs. It's a bit of a hellhole, all the truckers just piss out of their windows and chuck their rubbish and there's all sorts of wheeling and dealing and prostitutes hanging around and kids kicking balls against the bus and you're never sure if it will be a brick next. A noisy place, you can hear the power station all the time and sirens going off.

There was this girl I was keen on for a while, Polish lass, hell she was beautiful. Met her when she was working in the pub. Sometimes we'd have a drink or I'd show her places or she'd come back to the bus. Never took her down to the scrapyard though or to the docks. I knew I had to clean myself up a bit and get some money in my pocket if I was to stand a chance with her. So I started taking on a few jobs to earn some extra, didn't ask no questions, just worked on the cars the ways the guys told me to and they'd give me fifty quid and that would be that. It only happened once in a while and I wasn't really that bothered. But then these guys started pestering me to work for them all the time, they were real pond life. There was this guy who wouldn't leave me alone. When I parked in the scrapyard he used to beep my bus every morning and pester me and it was so annoying and I thought, right, I've had enough. So I got him in the brew room up against the wall and I said you don't mess with me and I had my fist back and I started laying into him but luckily the others dragged me off of him so he wasn't left too bad. I knew I was in trouble after that, you don't mess with them lot so I escaped back to the village. I hope they don't catch up with me. I keep moving around hoping they won't find me.

I've got nothing left in the system now, no bank account or no address. There's no job I particularly want to do. I could earn a lot of money working for those guys again but it's not worth it. When I was in the scrapyard they thought I was some new age traveller. I've never known anyone who lived on a bus; this is just something that I conjured up. Sometimes it's great but sometimes you're full of fear cos you can get moved on at any time and it's hard work, getting wood for the fire to keep yourself going. I've never met any of those people on the road. I've heard they are usually twats and up to no good, travelling around with no papers at night and having a party. I'm not into thieving though a lot of

95

them are – if you think about it it's one hundred per cent profit, the easiest crack in the world.

I like parking here by the river; it's a bit private and it's convenient. You can pop out for a pint or some milk and I have a wash in the river in the morning, chuck water over me, and you've got the sound of the river all the time. I built a fire pit down there, under the trees, and there's a big slab to cut up your food. I keep a bucket of river water under the bus where I keep my milk cool. If it's a really hot day, I change the water a couple of times. It's my favourite place at the moment but I keep moving in case those guys catch up with me.

I love waking up somewhere new. Gyppos live the longest because it's not good for your state of mind to stay in one place, naturally humans are travellers, hunting for miles. Some mornings you wake up and you're listening to the sounds for a brief second as you come round and you think, where have I parked? And you open the curtains and think, yeah, that's where I am.

There's all sorts of life out of these windows – if you listen you can hear the kingfishers coming and see them flying two foot above the river, they make a whistling noise sssszzzwwwtt as they go along. There's a squirrel who lives in that beech tree over there. He runs the same circuit every morning along the wall, rummages in the bin, jumps down onto the rocks, waits for me to get up and open the door. He sits on that stub of a branch for me to throw out the food.

One day the door was wide open and this little bird flew out of its nest over there on the embankment and into the bus, zigzagged down the bus and crashed into the windscreen at the front. I found it under all this stuff, put it on my finger and took it outside to the wall and tried to get it off my finger but it kept clinging to me. Its little claws gripped my finger and wouldn't let go. Eventually I got it on the wall and came back here and watched it through the back window. The mother swooped over and grabbed it up and flew away with it and I couldn't be sure what she did with it cos it smelt of me. I don't know whether she dropped it to death from the embankment or put it back into the nest.

I've got no plans. Everything that's happened has just happened. Like that girl I was in love with; she hangs around sometimes but then I don't see her for ages and I don't care. I've got all the time in the world, totally free now, no ties, no commitments and I could do anything but half the time I can't be arsed and just sit around here. I have this falling dream, and last week I had it so bad that I fell a great height and when I woke up I thought I really had fallen cos I hurt all over. If someone was driving down from Scotland to Spain and they pulled off the motorway looking for a chippie and they ended up parking next to me and they said, 'We're off to Spain, want to come?', then I probably would if they were alright. I'm just sitting here looking at the hills, watching the earth to see what will grow. I dunno.

The Month of Writing Dangerously
Clare Weze Easterby

The house is practically in the woods. *Snap it up*, Bridget thinks. *It won't be vacant for long.* 'It can't be much for that price,' her mother had said at the weekend. 'Probably just a damp room in an attic.' But her mother is about to be proved wrong. There's richness all around and she's only in the hallway. Marble tiles, a huge Art Deco mirror, even an umbrella stand in the shape of an elephant's foot. *Well appointed.*

The landlady walks ahead, leading the way, and Bridget struggles to keep the smile off her face. Mrs. Jones must be about sixty-five. She wears a kind of coatdress in lilac with amazingly detailed buttons. Her grey hair, styled in a flapper bob, is waved but the waves look natural rather than stiff. Old-fashioned, but somehow immensely fashionable. Odd that such a dumpy, busty older woman can look fashionable, but there it is.

'And this is the kitchen.'

99

It's huge, with white painted cabinets. The ones on the wall have glass windows, and inside them are china plates and cups. Bridget swallows. 'It's all very nice.'

Mrs. Jones makes a little noise of agreement in her throat. The cooker gleams. A row of glass jars sits on a shelf beside it. Bridget clutches her handbag and tries to sound confident. 'It's definitely self-contained?'

'Oh, yes. I have to come through to see to the geyser from time to time, because it's in that cupboard.' Mrs. Jones gestures towards a door leading off to their left. 'But there's nothing I can do about that.'

Bridget hardly takes this in. Her own kitchen! Not to mention a sitting room, with a three-piece suite and those luxurious velvet curtains, so thick she feels like wrapping herself up in them as she used to do as a child. Upstairs, things are just as good, if not better. The bed is large and the eiderdown thick and covered with pale green silk. Bridget trails a finger along the fabric.

'Regent Street,' says Mrs. Jones, watching Bridget's finger. 'A lovely shop with every kind of Chinese silk. It's not there any more.'

Bridget thinks, *If this is the standard for the tenant's annexe, what on earth might her own quarters be like?* There is a large wardrobe of some sort of dark, shiny wood—her father would be able to tell her what it was instantly—and a matching dressing table with brass-handled drawers. The window is again dressed in rich fabric, lighter and lacier than that downstairs, and in cream. The window is open and she peers outside. She can hear distant trickling water; there might be a lovely little stream in the grounds. 'It's beautiful,' she says.

'Hmm... this was my daughter's room.'

They complete the formalities in Mrs. Jones's part of the house, and it is indeed opulent. Stuffed with antiques, lacquered pieces, gilt mirrors and so much china and glass that Bridget, for all her slimness, moves gingerly in case she knocks anything over. Two cats arch and wind around Mrs. Jones's legs. One is grey with chunky hair, a fat face and nasty, weepy eyes. The other is a Siamese. Bridget, unmoved by them, watches curiously as Mrs. Jones handles them like precious children.

Mrs. Jones folds Bridget's cheque and squints at her. 'You've just finished college?'

'Yes. In May.'

'And landed a job already?'

'Yes—private secretary at Noble Hall.'

'Not bad for a first job. A step up from the typing pool.'

Bridget doesn't know what to say.

'I expect you're very good.' Mrs. Jones raises her eyebrows and smiles. 'You might see my Daily in the mornings. Mrs. Paterson.'

Bridget smiles, almost oblivious. She wants to go home and pack, the sooner to claim her own sitting room, her bedroom, her own kitchen.

'Mrs. P is my mainstay. You'll get used to her around the place.'

'Lovely,' says Bridget.

On her first morning, Bridget is woken early by clattering coming from the kitchen and goes downstairs in her dressing gown. A squat woman with straw-coloured hair is fetching a mop and bucket. Mrs. P. The cleaning equipment she'd noticed on her exploration is obviously communal.

'Oh. You are waken then. I was beginning to wonder.' Mrs. P frowns as she speaks. Her eyes are very wide and seem younger than the rest of her face, which looks fiftyish. 'I'll be five minutes. I've got to do out the back rooms this morning and the cats have made a scrow.' She stares at Bridget, weighing her up, and although Bridget towers above her, she feels at a nasty disadvantage.

'How d'you do,' says Bridget. Margaret, the girl who used to come and 'do' for her mother, was always meek and sweet and would never have looked at a person like this. It's practically baleful, almost as if Mrs. P is her superior. Which is ridiculous.

Home from work on the Friday of her first week, Bridget's mind is still ringing with the tasks she accomplished as her heels crunch on the gravel drive. She'll have to watch this or her shoes will be ruined, but she doesn't dare walk on the grass, with good reason as it turns out: Mrs. Jones emerges from behind a bush, dressed in gardening trousers.

'Do cut yourself some flowers whenever you like. Sweet peas are legion this year.'

'Thank you, Mrs. Jones.'

'How's the first week gone?'

'Oh, you know... settling in, but it's going to be okay, thank you.'

'Piling on the work, is he?'

'Well, there's always a rush. They seem to want everything done at once.'

'Hmm... wanting train journeys booked, catering organised, figures double-checked, meetings arranged—all those letters you have to do on top of it must seem like a luxury.'

Bridget is stunned. 'Have you?'

'No, I was never a secretary but my daughter's friends, you know.' Mrs. Jones waves a gloved hand and moves on to the next bed.

Bridget carries on around the back of the house where the path meets the gently rustling trees. She feels buoyant and summery. She's just walked past that young man with the really nice motor car who lives near the gates of Hornby Castle. *Cream, with shiny metal parts... must be brand new.* He looks an ordinary type too, so she wonders how on earth he comes to afford a motor car.

She sits on the sweetheart seat and stares up into the canopy, where captured sunlight seems to dangle. If it wasn't for the char lady, this place would be sheer perfection. Every morning when she comes down for breakfast, there is Mrs. P. Bridget has taken to eating breakfast with the radio in the sitting room, but one morning she opened the heavy drapes to find Mrs. P grimacing at her and rubbing the windows. It was eight a.m. Elvis was singing 'All Shook Up,' but that staring, disapproving face was spoiling it. Why did she need to start so early? Margaret never came to her mother's before nine. But there is *one* thing: she would make a great character in a novel. *Bridget's novel. A nasty character.* And one day soon she must get started on it.

Inside, the kitchen smells strongly of freshly ironed laundry. It's a marvellous smell, but she hates the feeling that her quarters have been used in her absence. Galvanised, she gets out her notebook and starts jotting: *A squat woman, envious in demeanour*, she writes, *with none of the grace of the serving classes.*

For a good week now she's made sure her evening walk includes the area next to the castle gates, but in the end, it happens when she's picking flowers in the field next to the woods. Wellingtons force the wearer to lengthen their stride, giving a confident, determined air, and it is this gait that alerts her. He's heading her way! The Motor Car Man!

She stands still and waits. The sun is low in the sky, casting a sweet-tempered orange light that makes strange shadows fall from the wood.

As he arrives, she lifts her head and smiles the smile she's practised. 'How do?' he says. 'Haven't I seen you walking round the village these last few days?'

Bridget's face fills with heat.

He balances the posts he's carrying so that his tanned forearms rest across them, hands relaxed.

A farmer. Her voice is breathless. 'Hello! Yes, I think I've seen you too. I'm Bridget.' She fiddles with her daisies and buttercups, her eyes darting from his wellies to his work shirt, then up to his straight blond hair. *Such thick hair... such a fine colour....*

'I'm David. There's a dance at the Institute on Friday.' He smiles shyly, then looks away up the meadow, still smiling, his eyes focusing on the spot near the wood where the grass is longest and a breeze dances.

Bridget stifles a shiver. 'Oh! That sounds nice.' She smiles. *Long eyelashes... almond-shaped eyes....*

'Can I take you?'

103

Her heart booms. 'Um... well, I suppose so!' she answers too soon and her breathing is misbehaving. She's had no preparation, but a delicious warm, proud feeling is taking over her whole body.

'Where shall I call for you?'

Bridget thinks. *I've fluffed my acceptance, so I'd better hold something back. Men like mystery. It says so in* Woman's Own. 'I'll meet you at the door,' she says, turning to go. She'll reveal her grand address to him later on, like a prized jewel.

'Half-past seven?'

She looks at the waving branches behind his head, then meets his eyes again. She nods.

Once out of his sight she mouths the sentences she's carrying home in her head: *The remarkable in the everyday....* If only she'd brought the notebook with her. She can't stop smiling. She'll surely smile every day now for the rest of her life. *Through half-closed eyes...*

She hasn't written anything for a couple of days, but where did she last have the notebook? She remembers seeing it in the sitting room on the coffee table, on the sofa cushion, in the *kitchen* beside the kettle... *No! Please, God, don't let it have been left in the kitchen!*

She turns the house upside down and tries to remember what she has written. There was a funny passage about the charlady dripping with the contents of one of her own upturned mop buckets. There was also the true account of Mrs. Jones bossing Mrs. P—which struck her as rare at the time—when Mrs. P used that long instrument to clean the front upstairs windows. 'They're black with mildew. They should not be allowed to become black.' She had written that *verbatim*, intending to change it later. If they find it there will be no mistaking who she's been writing about! She flops down on the settee and puts her face in her hands. Her underarms are dampening. Mrs. Jones likes her, likes having her as a tenant. The notebook, if they find it, will change all that. Mrs. P will show it to Mrs. Jones, oh yes she will, and she will enjoy every second of the showing.

She goes to work the following day without having found it. She rushes the ledgers and drinks too much coffee because she hasn't slept. At home, she dashes up the path in the hope that speed will stop Mrs. Jones from materialising in the garden. All is quiet.

She finds the notebook on the floor next to the airing cupboard after her bath. She would have walked past it half a dozen times, so somebody must have taken it and returned it to this spot—but then again, she walked past it just now on her way to bathe, so perhaps it's been there all the time.

She scribbles out all the identifying material but keeps the descriptions, because they're good. She changes the characters beyond recognition and decides to build up the romance to make that the main focus. With David's face in her mind she writes:

There were other surprises too, during their courtship. He had marvellous handwriting (a lovely, consistent slant) and could paint fine flowers in watercolours. Imagine that! A farmer! She loved that delicate art, that side of him. Even when he was manhandling a sheep or knocking in a fence post or doing any of the other capable, tough jobs he did every day, there was a gentle grace about him. She was smitten.

She puts the notebook into her dressing table drawer and slides a handful of stockings down on top of it. Never again will it leave this room!

It is the morning of the dance. Downstairs, the kitchen window is steamed up and there's a bowl of hot water in the sink. Bridget makes tea and toast and takes her time about it. She's not going to hide in the sitting room today. When Mrs. P comes back to the kitchen, Bridget is sitting on a stool by the back door, sipping tea. She faces Mrs. P and does not smile.

Mrs. P puts a pair of wooden laundry tongs into the sink with a bad-tempered clatter. 'Interesting letters you get to type at Noble Hall, then?' She stares at Bridget's nose, as if there's something sticking to it. Bridget has to pass a hand over it just in case.

'I don't just type letters. He runs an import/export business, so there's lots to arrange.'

Mrs. P is obviously one of those people who think secretarial work is easy. How hard can it be, typing a letter when you've been told what to type? Filing things alphabetically—simple, surely.

'Must be nice to get to sit down all day.' Mrs. P screws her eyes up and rubs at her forehead, as if trying to eradicate wrinkles. 'We never had opportunities like that. Going to fancy colleges.' Mrs. P wrings out her cloths, empties the basin and shuffles off into Mrs. Jones's quarters.

Bridget is speechless. Mrs. P reminds her of old Aunt Alice whom she'd had to visit every blessed Sunday. *Just exactly the same kind of disapproval.* She starts to open the parcel Mrs. P must have left on the side for her, then notices the address label. *Mrs. Florence Jones... stupid blind woman.* Bridget takes it through the joining door, following the cleaning noises Mrs. P makes as she moves through the house, which smells of lavender polish.

She finds Mrs. Jones in the kitchen. Little clouds of steam puff from the kettle, and Mrs. P unloads a stack of linen from a deep dresser next to the window. Bridget ignores Mrs. P.

Mrs. Jones is perturbed as there is no note inside the parcel and she knows nobody in Chicago. 'Oh, it's a scarf.' She drapes it across one arm and squints at it. 'Oh, feel this—the fabric is *so* fine.' Fabric seems to be the major love of her life.

Bridget touches the scarf. 'Is it cotton?'

'*Indian* cotton,' says Mrs. Jones, giving the shawl a shake. 'Of generous proportions.' She's wearing toreador pants and a grey linen jacket today. Bridget has never seen such pants on a person of her age. They are a rich blue that some might call purple, the most beautiful shade she has ever seen. She realises for the first time that fabric makes up for old skin. You can still be a thing of beauty, but your clothes must step up several notches so that they draw the eye, replacing what's lost. You could have fun being old if it allowed you to dress like this.

106

'I'm going to a dance at the Institute tonight. Haven't a clue what to wear.'

Mrs. P looks in their direction, but Bridget still ignores her. Mrs. Jones's eyes sparkle. 'Ah. In that case, come with me.' Mrs. Jones looks fierce and determined, as if she's on a serious mission, and Bridget follows her, still studiously avoiding Mrs. P.

'Something in tulle or silk,' Mrs. Jones says as they climb the stairs. 'Rose or mint, bring out the peaches in your cheeks.'

She gives her three outfits to choose from and, waving Bridget's thanks aside, leaves her alone in the large, overwhelmingly beautiful bedroom to try them on. Only the cats spoil the morning. They arrive suddenly, from nowhere, leaping on the bed and staring at her while she undresses. The grey one kneads the counterpane with its paws and the Siamese stands awkwardly, as if it's waiting for her to do something worth seeing before it commits to getting comfortable.

She wonders whether the clothes are Mrs. Jones's from her younger years, or her daughter's; the outfits seem so timeless that there is no way of telling. She chooses a delicate calf-length rose-coloured dress with a beaded V neckline. She can wear it with a scarf she bought in Edinburgh last year. The cats stare on, their gaze following her as she walks in front of the mirror. She changes, sticks her tongue out at them, then rushes back through the cool lavender rooms and gets her bag ready for work.

At six p.m. her hair is finished. Her mother always said she messed around with her hair far too much. Well, now she can mess around to her heart's content. She can have too many perms, cut it too short, even colour it! There's nobody to stop her! Except that the job demands a certain amount of propriety. It's been dawning on her over the last few weeks that she has to go there every day now, every week, for months and years on end. Dislike of that thought seeps through now and then, even though she tries to stop it, especially now in July when the long summer hols ought to be looming. There are compensations though. She has her own place. And at last, she has a bag with a clasp that snaps open and closed with a sharp click! There is nobody to ask her what time she'll be home or to tell her whom she really ought and

107

ought not to be seeing. She puts lipstick and powder into the bag and stands in front of the full-length wardrobe mirror for the last time, patting her hair and wondering whether she should have put it up after all.

The dance is noisier than she'd imagined. It's hard to talk. She hears her father saying, *That's why it's called a dance. It's not called a talk, is it?* She has to lean in close to hear David, which makes her heart beat far too fast.

'So where do you live?' he asks.

She has to speak loudly, almost shouting at him. 'That's for me to know and you to wonder.'

'You're not going to tell me?'

'No.'

'You're a rum 'un.' He grins at her. There is more in his face than his words are revealing. *Much more....* Then they start to play 'Bye Bye Love' and he asks her to dance. Afterwards they move out into the lobby and it's much easier to converse. People are noticing them together, which feels right. Bridget starts to talk about family, but then he tells her his father died twelve years ago.

'Right at the end of the war,' he says, and looks away.

'I'm so sorry,' says Bridget. The moment is excruciating, so she waxes lyrical and comical about the horrible char woman, whom she doesn't name, remembering chunks from her notebook, killing two birds with one stone: being witty and testing out her novelistic prowess. 'Battle lines have been drawn in the soap suds,' she says.

David listens. He smiles at the words, laughs at them, but he also smiles when she isn't talking. He smiles during the gaps and looks into her eyes. When they go outside at the end of the evening, he reaches for her and kisses her, long and slow.

'I'll walk you home,' he says, but she runs away by herself like Cinderella, leaving him standing at the side of the Institute.

Home, she sits at her dressing table and stares at her reflection. Her cheeks are glowing. Her hair has stayed in place and shines

108

like gold. Her lips ought to look different. She touches them with a fingertip, marvelling. Retrieving her notebook, she writes, *Wrapped in mystery and rose tulle, the village itself seemed mad with jealousy.* She puts the notebook safely back in the drawer, too lost in thinking about that kiss to carry on.

Bridget is almost at the church. She stops to look at a cloud of intense blue lobelia on somebody's doorstep, feeling the letter thick between her fingertips. She's early. David will be out at work, but still she posts it quickly and with stealth, just in case.

She imagines him reading the address, his reward after waiting a full week since the dance. He'll get out of his work things and come to her straight away—and she won't be there. She carries on walking, goes to a different place up the river bank, farther than she's been before, with her notebook, a paperback, a blanket and a little snack, feeling romantic. All week she's avoided the field where they met. She's been to Loyn Bridge, into Gressingham and even past the station and up towards the fells. She starts to read some poetry, but doesn't get far before daydreams take over again.

This extra hiatus will make him long for her even more. She pictures his mouth; his lips are unusually full and remind her of someone—a film star, though she can't remember which. She looks back at the castle and writes, *The Castle, once the central seat of the medieval lords of Hornby, now the dramatic backdrop to their meetings.*

She arrives home quite late, convinced he'll have been and gone.

The next day is Saturday; there's still no word. By mid-afternoon the sky has filled with grey clouds, partially obscuring the bright sun that lingers from morning, and Bridget is a little worried. Perhaps he's had to go somewhere. He'll come for her tonight and they'll swap their life stories. By evening the rain has come and she has been waiting in her sitting room, ready, not moving around too much for fear of creasing her linen trousers. She would have gone for a long walk today if she'd known. That's what she should have done. Now she's stiff and tired, high and dry and thinking of those girls whose boyfriends don't get in touch.

Even Mrs. Jones has gone out. She popped her head through the door and asked whether Bridget would mind looking in on the cats around eight o'clock or so. Bridget prowls through the cold, immaculate rooms. Some parts of the house are seldom used. The floors are still polished to a mirror-high shine, but it's strange how one can tell whether a room is lived in or not even when all are maintained equally.

Quite creepy, these empty rooms. She runs her fingers over the crimson velvet of a chair, then stops to look at all the photographs on the grand piano. Mrs. Jones's willowy daughter framed in mother-of-pearl. Probably taken before she married and moved to Dorset. Sleek dark hair and Mrs. Jones's hazel eyes. Mr. and Mrs. Jones together from long ago, framed in dark red lacquered wood. He's tall and bald, has a wry smile and a pipe in his hand. *How did he die? Wasn't it an accident?* She can't remember what kind. Then she spots a small bamboo-framed one of Mrs. Jones and Mrs. P standing in the garden together, grinning. She frowns and crosses her arms, bending closer. Judging by their hairstyles and faces, it's fairly recent. She shakes her head, surprised, and looks around the room. There's only the sound of rain dripping on leaves outside the window. There's no other sound.

She comes upon the cats in the sitting room. She's in her stockinged feet and has crept up on them successfully, and now they're paused in mid-wash, eyes wide. 'Silly creatures,' she says. 'I'm here. You have company.'

By Sunday her eyes have become fixed and there is no trace on her lips that she's ever smiled. The day drags. At some points, were it not for her watch, she would be totally unable to say whether it was morning or afternoon. Still reluctant to leave the premises, she goes over and over the dance, their kiss, their conversation, searching for clues that might confirm that she's had his personality wrongly pegged. There's time to write, but it feels pointless. The notebook hasn't moved from its drawer since

Friday night.

At six, she drags the ironing board out roughly and ploughs through the week's clothes.

On Monday morning, Bridget goes through into Mrs. Jones's kitchen. 'Sorry to disturb you Mrs. Jones; it's just that I've been expecting a note and wondered whether anything has been delivered to this side.'

Mrs. Jones is buttering toast and obviously trying to do it as cleanly as possible, but drops a butter-smeared knife and crumbs fall all over the worktop like snow. 'Dammit!' She bends for the knife. 'No my dear, I haven't had anything besides the usual, I'm afraid. No Mrs. P today either—she has the doctor calling this morning.'

'Oh.' Bridget pauses. She doesn't like to ask what might be wrong. Then again, it seems rude not to. While she's dithering there's a sharp needling on her leg. She flinches. A cat is underfoot. It bats the fringing on her skirt and she takes a sideways step. It's the Siamese.

'Well well,' says Mrs. Jones. 'I think Jade is trying to cause a little mischief.' She's wearing a jet necklace today. Bridget can't keep her eyes off it. 'Would you be a dear and drop these blooms in to Mrs. P on your way? She lives in the row of cottages just this side of the castle entrance. Her son's car is usually outside, a cream Austin A30. The house with the red door.'

Bridget says nothing. Her cheeks are burning.

'Drizzle forecast again today,' says Mrs. Jones. 'Not entirely a bad thing for the garden.'

The grey cat is kneading the rug, dribble gathering at the sides of its mouth. The Siamese is out of sight. Bridget feels her leg stinging where its claws broke the skin. Mrs. Jones grandfather clock strikes eight as she remembers what she said and wrote. *A hag... his mother.*

Bridget reaches out slowly, takes the freesias and walks out of the house with her handbag on her shoulder. She realises now why his mouth was so familiar and feels faint. The fruit and veg man passes her in the drive and winks, as usual, before his eyes

111

settle on the crimson of her face and neck. 'Cheer up love—it might never happen!'

A bird descends from the branches behind his van, seeming to float on the air, and in the village, the main business of the morning gets underway.

Exile on High Street
Clare Weze Easterby

They call us the Boys on Bikes—Nat, Kyle and Alex (that's me) and Harry (when his mum lets him). And this was the weirdest day we'd ever had.

We were bored riding up and down so all four of us stopped outside the village hall to squeeze our tyres and check the street was behaving. That's when we first saw the blue van drive past the church and park outside the shop. We didn't know that van, so we watched and waited. Nobody got out. Nobody was shopping. The driver was watching people—we could tell.

'Hey,' Nat said. 'Let's investigate.' So we rode up to the shop, parked our bikes and went inside for more penny sweets, but they were just for cover. We eyeballed the van man while we stood in the queue. He wasn't that old. Boring jacket and shirt, like a teacher, but he was no teacher. Cool haircut, uncool scabby van. Brown hair, thick dark eyebrows and a stud in the ear we could see.

I whispered to the lads, 'Van, haircut and jacket—none of it goes together.' They looked at him, then back at me and I felt like a genius.

Outside, we circled him while he pretended to stare at the tins of beans and loaves of bread and fruit and marmalade painted on the shop front. A man walked past with a Great Dane; Van Man watched him. Someone's dad came out of the shop with a guitar on his back; Van Man watched him too, as if he was memorising everyone. He eyeballed Kyle, and Kyle's arms froze in a funny position, like he was stunned.

'Freaky!' Kyle muttered to the rest of us, and we rode away, back to the village hall and sat on our bikes with our feet on the ground.

'Right. This is Position One,' I said. 'The shop's Position Two.'

'We're not just the Boys on Bikes,' said Kyle. 'We're the Guardians of Burton!'

'Yes!' said Nat.

'Brave,' I said. 'Fearless.'

'Noticing everything!' said Kyle.

'Missing nothing!' said Harry with his mouth full of chocolate. 'We'll protect the shop from shoplifters.'

I felt as if my head might lift right off. 'We'll stop fights. We'll even stop arguments!'

But there was no more time for planning because Van Man was getting out of his van... and walking up the street... and knocking on Nat's grandad's door!

'I knew he didn't look right,' said Nat. We hurried over but there was a car coming so we weren't fast enough: he was inside before we even reached the kerb. We dumped our bikes in the front garden, dived for the door and knocked hard.

Nat's grandad opened the door, looked over his shoulder at Van Man, turned back to us boys and scratched his head. 'Now then, lads, I've got a visitor so I can't have all of you trooping in. Nat, take your friends round the back and wait quietly.'

We went round and the back door was open. We didn't all

116

fit into the tiny kitchen; Kyle and Harry spilled out into the garden. He needn't have bothered telling us to be quiet; we were like statues. We were like listening machines, our whole bodies tuned in and the lot of us might as well have been joined together to make one gigantic ear. This is what we heard:

'A *Dorothy* Green you say?' Nat's grandad asked. 'Anyone who might remember her?'

'Yes. My great-grandmother,' said Van Man. He sounded slimy. 'She lived in Burton until around 1945. When the chap down the road said you were a Green, I wondered....'

'That's something I've *always* intended to do, look up the family tree. Never got round to it. How far back have you got?'

'Not too far as yet, but I'm interested in getting the feel of the area.' Now he sounded like someone on a TV advert trying to sell some old rubbish. 'My gran lived in Burton till she was about ten. I was weaned on the stories she told me about his village.'

Nat's eyes opened so wide I thought they might pop, and when his grandad went to fetch some old photos from the bedroom, we crept right up to the lounge door, squeezed together and spied in through the cracks. Van Man looked around the room, staring at the telly and the radio, narrowing his eyes at the old brass above the fireplace. He gave the room a good going over, but that wasn't what made our hearts start thumping out of our chests. It was his face. It was hard and determined, like he was doing a job. And as soon as he heard Nat's grandad's feet on the stairs, his face changed back to ordinary.

Nat's grandad had a ton of papers and photos in his arms. 'There's a few second cousins of my mother's that might be possibilities.'

Nat looked at me and shook his head. 'This isn't right,' he mouthed. I widened my eyes back at him and put my face back to the crack. The kitchen smelt of tea and lino.

'Here's one of my mother. And this is an aunt, taken at Mount Wellington. Burton used to have a lot of potteries, you know. Your gran will have told you that.'

'Yes,' said Van Man. His face! It was all slimy nodding, but he blinked far more than he smiled. 'She moved to Warwick in the forties. My mum was born there and so was I.'

Nat's grandad sat in his chair and the photos spilled all over his legs. 'Are you still there?'

'No, I stayed in Bangor after university. I'm in the marine biology department now.'

'Now that is quite a coincidence. Because I was only reading this morning—this morning, mind you—about something that's right up your street. "The Blind River Dolphin." He rolled the r in river and we all smirked. He reached down behind his chair and pulled out a magazine. 'It's in this *National Geographic* here. Look at that.'

'Ah,' said Van Man. He took the magazine and glanced over it really fast. '*Platanista gangetica minor.* The Indus river dolphin.'

'That'll be its Sunday name,' said Nat's grandad. 'Their eyes don't work.'

Van Man was quiet, reading again. His face was a bit red. He looked like Jake Deacon had when Mr. Hindle caught him cheating in a test. 'Yes,' he said. 'No functional lens, but they may be able to distinguish light intensity and direction.' He just read that straight off the page; you could tell he didn't really know anything about dolphins.

'Well, you could have sent me to the bottom of our stairs, because I'd never heard of the creatures,' said Nat's grandad. 'And I like fish.'

'Mammals,' said Van Man.

'What's that?'

'The dolphin is a mammal.'

'Yes, but fancy a dolphin living in a river!' Nat's grandad's voice went up high when he said 'river'. We all looked at each other and started that shoulder shaking silent laughing thing that gets you detention at school. Here, it would get us thrown out of the house, so we looked at the floor and put our hands over our noses and mouths till it died down, which took ages.

Van Man smoothed the magazine over his knees and put a clever expression on his face. His elbows were on the arms of the chair and his fingers were pushed together like a church steeple, like he'd seen someone do that on telly, perhaps on QI or something. 'Yes, that always seems to be a surprise.'

'And having poor sight,' Nat's grandad went on. 'You'd wonder how it gets around. How it finds food.'

'Echolocation.'

'Well yes, but I mean, you'd want something more than that, wouldn't you, underwater.' We couldn't see Nat's grandad's face, but we guessed he was staring at Van Man. 'And you'd wonder why these things happen to the wretched creatures.'

'Really good sonar equipment they've got, dolphins.'

'Yes, but you'd wonder why they didn't have good eyes as well. Because then they'd be able to manage twice as easily.' He stood up and turned, and now we could see him, see his eyebrows lifted up in amazement. 'A cup of tea now, I think.'

We scrambled back outside. We made it in time, but only just. We went further down the garden where they wouldn't hear us.

'He's not related to me, isn't that man,' said Nat.

'He could be a gunman,' said Kyle. 'The Doctor would just shout, *Run*!'

Nat snorted. He doesn't watch *Doctor Who*. 'So how are we going to get him away from my grandad?'

'Your grandad's sussed him,' I said. 'Look how he got him onto whales and dolphins!'

'But what if he really is a dolphin expert?' said Harry. We might have known. Harry's mad on whales and dolphins.

'Don't be mental,' I said. 'He's a con artist.'

Nat's grandad came down the garden path carrying a tray of blackcurrant juice. 'All right, lads?'

We all nodded, but we were standing funny, like we were dying to get back to listening in. We took our drinks and said thank you.

'Grandad!' said Nat. 'That man's bad!'

His grandad just gave us a grin and went back inside with the empty tray, so we didn't know what to think. When we went back to the door and listened again it was all about the olden days and this relative and that granny and some old aunty, and it went

119

on and on and on. We couldn't stand it for long. Nobody could've.

We met up again after tea and biked to our den on the road to Spiderweb Gates. It's secret so I can't reveal the exact location, but have you noticed how spooky Burton Wood can be? That's a clue. But guess who we saw going past our den towards Clifford Hall? Van Man!

'Come on!' shouted Nat, and away we went.

It took us a few minutes, but we found him, parked up in that gateway that you think is going to be Spiderweb Gates, but it isn't, it's too soon. We came to a wobbly stop, left our bikes in the long grass at the edge of the road and crept along on foot.

'Careful,' I said. 'We can't blow our cover.' The unseen Guardians.

We watched. 'He's got a camping stove!' said Nat. 'He's going to sleep in his van!'

Wow! I felt like I might burst. Van Man was a kind of tramp; a tramp with a van. He got the stove going. The back of the van was open and there was a lot of stuff in there. 'Wish we were a bit closer,' I said.

Harry narrowed his eyes. 'Sleeping bag, camping stuff...'

'That's a hot water bottle!' said Kyle. 'So's that! He's got loads of them!'

Harry frowned at him. 'He's got three.'

'Yeah, loads!'

'He's eating his tea,' said Nat.

We waited. I found a stone and scraped off all its moss.

'He's smoking a fag,' said Nat.

A bird fluttered out of the hedge close to Harry, making him jump. Then he raked all his fingers through his hair really hard and sighed. 'This is boring. He's not doing anything.'

'Well, what d'you want him to do?' I asked.

Nat stepped sideways into the verge. 'I bet he's frauded someone, like he's trying to fraud my grandad. It won't work though. Grandad'll just talk him to pieces.'

'I bet he's a murderer,' said Kyle.

Harry scratched his head again. 'I bet he's just a bloke in a

120

van.'

'Do you want to be a guardian or not?' said Kyle.

Harry sniffed. 'I bet he's just someone who knows loads about whales and dolphins.'

We all looked at him.

'You'd go up to him, wouldn't you, if we weren't here,' said Kyle, shaking his head. 'You'd try to get him to talk about that stuff.'

Harry's mouth dropped open and he blinked and blinked. 'Huh! I would not! I'm not that stupid.' He looked at me as if I'd back him up, but I just shrugged.

Then suddenly, I remembered something. 'Hey, we haven't written down his registration!'

Kyle kept his eyes on the van. 'Got a pen?'

None of us had one so everyone tried to memorise it.

'We're going to need notepads and pens from now on,' I said.

Kyle nodded. 'Just pens, Alex. We can write everything on the back of our hands. Saves space.'

We concentrated while flies buzzed around us, but Van Man didn't move. It was boring and we fidgeted—Nat stroked a massive bruise on his arm, Harry pulled out strands of long grass and chewed them—but it was the biggest adventure we'd had. None of us knew what he was—gunman, conman, derelict, weirdo—and all of us were a little bit scared, but we kept remembering we were the Guardians and that made us brave.

The Guardians.... I said the words over and over in my head and they felt good. My mum calls us Boys Without Coats, but she hasn't got a clue about what it's like on these streets. Like the time we saw that cat being dumped by the river. Car drove up, opened door, put sack on ground and drove off. A cat crawled out of the sack and didn't know where it was. A tame cat. We all stroked it but Harry took it home 'cause the rest of our mums would've gone mental. But just imagine if we hadn't be there, patrolling? What would have happened to the poor thing? There are some nasty people in the world; my granny always says that and she's right. So we patrol on our bikes to make sure. That's all

121

we do—we make sure—and now we had our new name.

Soon it was close to bedtime. The wind started to blow and we watched it stir the branches above the van.

'This is taking ages,' moaned Harry, but as soon as his words were out, we heard a door slam: Van Man was on the move.

'Helmets on!' said Kyle. 'Into position!'

The van drove away and we could see stuff coming out of the exhaust. It was loud. We heard him brake and turn round, then come back towards Burton. *Towards us*. We shrank into a gateway. We knew what to do, all of us, without telling each other; we were a real team.

'After him!' said Kyle.

We set off at top speed. It was a downhill race and I kept my eyes straight ahead, the wind cold on my forehead and cheeks. We were doing great, keeping him in sight, until Harry stopped us with a battle cry. 'Hey! Look!'

'What?' screamed Kyle.

Harry had stopped pedalling. 'I saw it!'

'Saw what?' said Nat.

'The panther! The Panther of Burton!'

Nat stopped his bike. 'Where? Where?'

'Where?' Kyle stopped too, and me last of all.

'Over there, look! Just by the riverbank, it's going into those bushes now. Quick! Look!'

We looked and looked, hearts thumping like mad. The banking was dark and shadowy, full of green growth, but nothing moved.

'Can't see anything,' said Kyle.

Nat jerked his front tyre up in the air. 'Where's it gone?'

'It was there,' said Harry. 'It was massive. I'm telling you, it was that panther. It's true.' His face was white and his eyes were staring.

Nat started laughing at him. 'You sure it wasn't a dolphin in the river, Mate?'

We all laughed. 'Yeah,' I said. 'One of those river dolphins! Very rare, those!'

122

Harry glared at me. 'Shut up.'

'Come on,' said Kyle. 'We've lost him now!' And off we went again, faster than we'd ever dared along the river road and over Greta Bridge. We rode up Burton Hill till we had to push the bikes and I was thinking about the village, all of it, *our* bridge, the houses clinging to *our* hill, *our* massive church and mega-pointy steeple, *our* gigantic walls holding in *our* churchyard, *our* Castle Hill and *our* shop with *our* sweets and everything else we need from the nice shop people. *Our* nice shop people, who might be in danger from Van Man any second now! It made me pedal faster.

We found the van parked outside the shop again. We cycled towards it. We circled it, pretending to look in the shop window, but the van was empty. Van Man was gone, let loose in the village.

'He could be anywhere,' said Nat.

Someone carried a sobbing toddler out of the shop and Kyle stepped aside. 'You only park here if you're going to the shop. He doesn't know that.'

We took our chance and had a nosy through the van windows.

'Tobacco,' I whispered. 'And matches.'

Kyle peered in from the other side. 'Hot water bottles, blanket, maps.'

'And rubbish,' said Harry. 'Loads.' We looked at the Coke cans and sandwich wrappers, the instant soup and Golden Syrup Cake packets. We laughed.

'Come on, we've got to keep on mission,' said Kyle. 'Keep knowing where he goes.'

'Back to my grandad's I bet.'

We set off on our bikes again, down Duke Street. No sign of Van Man, but we kept our ears and eyes open so we'd miss nothing. This village looks calm, but if you look and listen properly it's full of stuff happening, even stuff you can't see like information travelling across all the wires and beaming from satellites. My brother told me that and he got it from his university.

123

We pushed the bikes up Chapel Lane and there he was, halfway up and looking into somebody's window. We passed him. Then we rode round again, and again, and again, circling him until he got to the top of the lane and crossed over High Street. He was heading round the back of Nat's grandad's.

Nat squeezed his brakes until they squealed. 'Quick! He's going in the garden!'

We followed, then ditched our bikes on the pavement and ran down the path.

'What's he doing?' asked Kyle.

We watched from the gate. Mr. Brown from next door came out; we could see his head bobbing about over the garden fence as he watered something.

'We'd better call the police!' said Kyle. 'Tell your grandad!'

'Wait!' I said. 'He's going in the shed! He's hiding!'

Nat gasped. 'Key's been left in the padlock again. I'll get Grandad.' He ran round to the front door but came back to us a moment later with his eyes bulging. 'The car's gone! Grandad's *out*!'

We stared at the shed halfway down the long narrow garden. We couldn't believe it. He really was hiding in Nat's grandad's garden shed. And next, we really were creeping through the garden and we really were locking him in it. Nat fed the padlock into place, Kyle steadied it while he pressed it down, Nat slid the key out of the bottom, I kept a lookout and Harry just stood there with eyes like saucers. We were fast and we were nearly silent. We rocked.

The weirdest thing was, Van Man didn't make a move to stop us and he didn't try the door. He just stayed silent. Hiding.

We looked at each other, not knowing what to do. Nat signalled with his head and we crept right down to the bottom of the garden and crouched on the damp grass.

'We got him!' I said. 'We've caught a criminal!' I grinned round at them all and they grinned back, but after a moment, Kyle shook his head and stared at me with wide eyes.

'Yeah, but... what are we going to do now? We'll have to call the police,' he turned to Nat. 'Or at least tell your grandad

124

when he gets back, Nat.'

Nat stared at the key in his hands.

'But we did it!' I said.

Kyle rubbed his hands together slowly. 'We'll be in trouble for locking him in,' he said. 'We've got to think.'

I thought about being locked in. It would smell of old cut grass and oil and metal tools. 'Why isn't he banging the door down? That's what I'd do.'

'He doesn't want to be found. He knows he shouldn't be snooping around Grandad's garden.'

'Perhaps he's waiting for us to go away,' said Kyle. 'Perhaps he can see us through a crack.'

We all stared at the shed and my heart started beating faster than ever. The wind blew again, a low down, rasping wind that lifted leaves and tiny bits of gravel.

I looked at Nat, then Kyle. 'We can't stop guarding it though, can we?'

Everyone shook their heads and Kyle took a deep breath. 'We should go and tell someone at the shop. They might tell us what to do.'

'Won't he have a mobile?' said Harry.

We all looked at each other, but nobody said anything for a moment. Then Kyle sighed and pulled at the bottom of his T-shirt. 'Yep,' he said. 'He will. Bound to. And he'll just ring other criminals to get him out... worse ones, probably.'

We thought about that for a few minutes. Kyle stretched his legs and stuck his hands in and out of his pockets. Nat didn't take his eyes off the shed. Sweat itched my forehead. Then I stood up and said, 'We'll have to let him out.'

It was a dangerous operation, perhaps the most dangerous the Guardians of Burton had ever carried out. Harry and Kyle waited at the garden gate, ready to run. Nat and me crept up to the shed and Nat undid the padlock.

As soon as it was unlocked we sprang away, like it was hot or wired up to the electricity. Then we got our bikes, dived across the road to the village hall and, gasping for breath, watched from behind the gates. We were just in time; there he was, hurrying onto High Street. He reminded me of a wasp. His head stayed in one place when he walked, like he was holding it super-straight. He didn't look at us once.

'We could have kept him there till morning,' I said. 'Taught him a lesson. Taught him to leave Burton alone.'

'I think he's going,' said Nat.

He was right. Van Man got into his van and raced out towards the school, way faster than the speed limit—and we biked after him. We pedalled like Daleks were after us, breathing hard and following, and he got behind something slow otherwise we'd have lost him for sure. He overtook it just before the school corner, and we reached the school just in time to see him leave the village.

'Going, going,' said Nat. We watched the blue van till it disappeared and all we were left with was the tarmac road dipping and turning out of Burton like spilt ink. 'Gone.'

We stayed there for a few minutes to make sure, then rode back towards the village, slowly, not saying anything or looking at each other at all.

Then Harry stopped his bike and made a funny humming noise. He pointed, and we all looked to where slices of sunset were shining between the clouds and lighting on something moving, something curling around the iron gate at the bottom of Castle Hill. It disappeared into the shadows: the long fat tail of something like a very, very big cat.

A Guide to Living and Working in the Museum
Clare Weze Easterby

In most cases you will be travelling alone and will arrive at the museum many thousands of kilometres from your home in surroundings that will at first seem alien. There will be villages surrounded by fields. This novelty alone will disorient you and although the specimens speak English, many phrases will have a different meaning from the norm.

You will not be met at the pod-port and must therefore follow the directions given to you by your line manager. The pavements in the villages are made of early concrete and are not self-cleaning. Any spillages will need to be removed by hand. You will be living in a Cottage with rudimentary hygiene facilities. This accommodation is less sophisticated than you are accustomed to, which may magnify trivial problems. There are usually Stairs, which must be negotiated with caution. There are no facilities for crushing and cubing waste; instead, all containers must be placed in the appropriate barrel for collection by mobile disposal unit.

You have been chosen for this role because you have demonstrated strong communication skills and a flexible attitude, but we ask you not to integrate with the specimens immediately. Proceed with caution until you have gained their trust and be prepared for shocks whilst you are acclimatising.

Each region of the Lune Valley has specific rules and regulations which must be adhered to at all times for your own safety. For example, in Hornby, Melling and Wray villages you may use your magnetic streamer but you cannot dance in the sunlight. Bentham, Burton in Lonsdale and Arkholme have more relaxed rules about sun-dancing, but rain-showering is strictly forbidden in all areas, even at the summit of the highest hills. Do not tamper with the minerals in any way.

In the small town of Kirkby Lonsdale, mixing with the specimens is prohibited. Should you feel the need to participate in leisure activities, you are obliged to leave this village in the evenings and search for them elsewhere. Specimens in all sectors must be treated with unreserved respect and deference at all times.

Communication: Three counties meet within the Lune Valley. You will therefore encounter a dialect containing Yorkshire, Lancashire and Cumbrian influences. Some phrases are converged en masse and individual words are extended. Others have numerous meanings. Some examples are as follows: **Starved** can mean to lack food or to suffer a lowered body temperature; **Happen** can mean that something has taken place, but it can also mean **maybe**; **While** can also mean **until**; **Fast** can mean stuck as well as **speedy**. Needless to say, misunderstandings can easily result. You must listen for the familiar word embedded in the dialect word.

Common examples:

Lookster = Look, will you

Is-ta = Are you

Can-ta = Can you

Will-ta = Will you

Has-ta = Have you

Meals should be eaten in your Cottage, in private. Under no circumstances should you allow yourself to be in a position where a specimen can view your food consumption. Full utilisation of the window coverings is requested. Alternatively, you may take meals to the first floor. The food will be authentic and you must take your probiotic tablets daily to prevent illness. Your medication will prevent the total rejection of fats in a form you have never ingested before, animal protein, 'dairy products' and the heavy sugar content, but be prepared for discomfort at first and eat slowly. You may drink freely in all areas.

Your uniform of Trousers, Shirt and Jacket must be worn at all times. Please ensure that they are kept clean and smooth. Remember that primitive laundry facilities rely on water and detergent: there are no UV air cleaning units. There are seasons in the valley and you will need to follow the corresponding dress code, adding and removing garments as necessary. Your system will take time to adjust to the constantly fluctuating temperature.

You will be expected to participate in all sampling and laboratory-based activities of the Unit, including the supervision and maintenance of equipment and prompt notification to your line manager in the event of malfunction (a routine problem in the village of Bentham). Data input should be completed at the end of each day and audit preparation for each research project should be completed weekly.

It is your own responsibility to remain updated on

changes in Health and Safety and Risk Assessment directives. The Lune Valley is a dangerous place. Your alarm must be accessible at all times and you must not venture into wild areas unaccompanied. Livestock may look benign but cows (*Bos primigenius*) and sheep (*Ovis aries*) carry microbes with which you are unfamiliar and have been known to charge, particularly when protecting young. When sampling, you will wear safety suits at all times and travel in pairs. In the wooded areas of the valley there may be other ruminant mammals, with antlers, although sightings of these at close proximity are extremely rare.

Despite appearances, the mountain known as Ingleborough is not suitable for power-pack charging. Regular emergency drills take place in the village of Caton and you are expected to attend these at least twice per tour.

In order to avoid a repeat of the incident in Sector 1149, Hornby Park Wood is now a restricted area.

~

Reading through the guide again, it is easy to see where we went wrong.

After a week acclimatising, Pedra and I reached a level of curiosity that we could no longer disregard; so we went to Kirkby Lonsdale. We ended up in a tiny room that served intoxicants and 'snacks'. It was only spring, but the females wore few clothes. Clearly overdressed in our 'shirts' and 'trousers', Pedra and I took the trousers off, the better to blend in. We thought we could sit in a corner of the room and speak to nobody except the service specimens. Sunlight streamed in through the glass doors. It felt good to sit swimming in the light, indulging in the atmosphere of days gone by. But remaining invisible was harder than we thought. Before long, a group of young men had edged towards us, looking in awe, appearing deeply fascinated by our legs.

'Perhaps we removed the wrong garment, Calia,' whispered Pedra. 'I'm going to go outside and put the trousers back on. I'll take off the shirt instead.'

We took turns at this, but the young men did not stop staring. It was not an entirely unpleasant sensation once we had got used to their unpredictable movements – leaning against walls, balancing one knee on a chair, slapping each other around the shoulders – and their flamboyant exchanges on subjects that could not be deciphered.

Pedra and I had become friends immediately as we negotiated the quaint vehicles and the peculiar washing facilities in the Cottage. We were equally intrigued by this ancient, mysterious world. I sipped my fruity refreshment beverage, giggling as it fizzed on my tongue, while Pedra smiled at the boys. I leaned across the table. 'Pedra,' I said, 'be careful. We cannot interact.'

'The guide does not say why though, does it? What is so different about these specimens? They look just the same as those we have already seen in Caton and Halton and that other little place – Wennerington?'

'Wennington. Pedra...'

'Perhaps there are secrets here. Perhaps we would never want to leave them.'

'Pedra! This is a wild place, remember!' The boys became louder, jostling each other and drowning out the music with their raillery, which often seemed to focus on human body parts.

Pedra looked warm and flushed, as if excited by the exotic display, but I felt I was beginning to understand their behaviour. It was almost certainly related to the way the females tottered around on spiked shoes in the evenings throughout the valley. This ritual was loosely related to what Pedra and I would call a dance and was probably density-dependent – the building was becoming crowded. I edged my seat further into the corner, but Pedra didn't follow my lead. Before I could warn her, the two closest boys brought their fists down on each other's heads in a mock fight. I flinched and made to get up.

'Relax,' Pedra soothed, 'they are competing with each *other*. They are harmless.'

A round-faced boy turned to face us as I sat back down again. He was breathing heavily, arms folded and head to one

133

side. 'Barbon Hillclimb at t' weekend, ladies,' he boomed. 'How d'you fancy it? Bikini weather's been given.' He laughed and turned away without waiting for an answer.

Pedra and I frowned at each other.

'With the bends and the hairpin?' the boy went on to his friends, 'you're joking. I could do it in a Ferrari. Or a Zonda. I could do it in Matt's Astra with her dressed like that – wham!' He clapped a hand on the shoulder of the boy next to him. 'Aston Martin Trophy *thank*-you-very-much!'

Hardly any of these words were recognisable and we couldn't assume a normal meaning for those that were.

'Perhaps there is another disease they wish to cure,' I suggested. 'That is the meaning of their sacrificial Sponsored Runs, is it not?'

Pedra shook her head doubtfully. 'No, this is different. I think the climbing takes place in vehicles – I recognise the language. Another superstition must be at work. Or perhaps it is an advancement. There is talk of *The Sun*. The dark-haired one mentions it often. "When we were in t' Sun", he keeps saying. It can only mean streaming solar particles.'

Pedra looked convinced but I shook my head at her. 'With what technology?'

'They already have the rudiments of rain-showering in the Happy Mount Park place we saw on the map. The spot marked 'splash pool'. Remember?'

'I'm not sure we were right about that, Pedra.'

For the next hour we sat and watched. I focused on what happened at the point of service while Pedra examined the behaviour of the boys. People hovered at the bar waving notes of currency; the servers laughed and talked while they created the coloured liquids and exchanged words and smiles with each transaction – often the same words. I stepped across the room briefly and took a recording and these bonding ritual words were repeated: *Hiya; No worries; There you go; Ice? Thanks love; Ta.* Then I returned to our table. To my horror, Pedra was telling one of the boys where we were staying.

'We've got grazing over there. We'll be moving some stock

134

into t' summer meadow before so long. If you look out your bedroom window at about four in t' morning one of these days, you'll see us. You can gis a wave! Perhaps I'll pop in for a cuppa tea.'

'Pedra!' I hissed.

'Wild, you said.' I did not like the change in her voice as she said this. And the day was passing; the pool of sunlight had abandoned us.

'Pedra, it is time!'

She ignored me. She seemed able to converse with them easily. '*No offence?*' I heard her say. '*I'm not being funny, but?*' I do not think she grasped the idioms at all, but it did not seem to matter: the boys continued to laugh and talk with her. '*Well fair play to you too!*' '*I am very brisk today, thank you.*' And then her voice and theirs blended into one mirthful fog.

'I will leave this place without you,' I said, standing. I should perhaps have been more forceful before this point, but we had only been working together for a few days. I walked towards the door and heard one of the boys call out to me, 'Bigger fish to fry, have you love?'

Pedra called out too. 'Chill ya beans, Calia!'

I will probably never know the meaning of this peculiar phrase, but she hurried after me so it must have been a declaration of defeat. It was still daylight outside but dusk was gathering in the corners. I said nothing, but my accusing glances stirred her.

We left Kirkby Lonsdale before nightfall.

Another working day. The old road wound a dark grey line between the endless patchwork of walled grassland, in and out, up and down, until one down-span dipped steeply between dwellings and we found ourselves at Bentham Auction Mart. The hills we came through were some of the prettiest I have seen, and the village itself felt raw and untouched; un-sampled, as if Pedra and I might be one of the first.

There was a river below the auction ground, and a field set aside for playing games. So many trees, all untouched – it was miraculous. I will never forget the trees, or the auction animals. No wonder the twenty-first century poets gathered here. The animals were being transported in the most curious wagons and trailers with their little eyes peeping out. They travelled in from three directions, one of the lanes so narrow that the carriages almost touched each other as they bumped along. It was all so quaint.

Pedra and I split up at the entrance. An earthy, romantic smell hit me as soon as I found Sector 1156, and I rubbed my arm where it was still tender from the extra antimicrobial shot I had had that morning. Judging from the smell, the microbial load was high.

I filtered into the crowd and settled next to a family, a father and two daughters. They were all pale-haired and sturdy, as if hewn from the landscape. The father was scolding the younger child and I opened my sampler to catch his groans.

'Give up mithering! Right, stay there. Megan, you're in charge.' He brushed past me as he left the stall and I was able to take a focused reading. His dissatisfaction level was high.

The older one caught my eye and I smiled sympathetically. She looked about twelve in years. Her younger sister remained restless. 'Is there actually a real Snow Queen?' she asked, her voice close to a whisper.

'I don't know,' replied the older one, 'there might have been once, but probably not any more. Stop asking or he'll just say no.' She turned to me. 'She wants to go and see The Snow Queen on Ice in Kendal.'

I leaned across her and smiled at the little girl. I too had seen the billboards for this pageant. I had been imagining it as a parade, but how would they freeze the surfaces of the town adequately? 'I hope your dream comes true,' I said, watching their father work at herding the dawdling cows through their gates. One of them slipped and his eyes widened, his hands seeming to spasm in the air in front of him in that tight moment before the animal recovered its footing.

'Waken up!' he commanded. I had been holding my breath. I forgot all about net productivity and total biomass. Living,

136

eating, growing, dying: all are supposed to equal the passage of energy in particles from sun to plant to animal to human to microbe, but his face made a nonsense of it.

'He's cross because we're going out of milk,' the older one said. She had been watching me staring at her father.

'What does that mean?'

She fiddled with her hair. 'We're not milking cows any more. All the cows are having to go.'

'Oh. Why is that?'

She sighed. 'It's the milk price.'

'The milk price?'

She shook her head and frowned at me. 'The milk price is terrible, so we're going out of milk. Those are our bulling heifers over there.'

I looked across at the animals, now passing smoothly through the holding cubicle and into the ring. I nodded. The little girl bobbed and fidgeted, peeping shyly at me and buffeting her sister, who was eyeing me carefully. 'You don't know what bulling heifers are either, do you?'

I laughed. 'I need a teacher.'

'You sound a bit different,' she said matter-of-factly. I drew a deep breath. 'Are you from Poland?'

I released the breath. 'Somewhere like that.'

'What's your name?'

'Calia.'

'That's nice. I'm Megan. I could translate for you,' she shrugged her shoulders and looked away, as if it did not matter. 'Which words don't you understand?'

'Ah, many words, many words. I have noted much, but now, let me think... oh yes. *Dab hand*.'

'Dab hand,' she pursed her lips, and frowned. 'Well ... you're at dab hand at something if you're good at it.'

'Thank you. What about *Fettle*?'

'Fettle. That's when you sort something out, really. You fettle it when you master it. Or it can be when you mend something. It's something my grandad would say. Young people don't talk like that.'

I nodded. I would not use that word to blend in. '*Had up.*'

'Oh, that's getting into trouble. A policeman comes and you have to go to court.'

I nodded, fascinated. '*Moider.*'

She giggled. 'That's pestering. This is good fun! Moider's like mither – it's what Emma was doing to my dad just now – mithering on about The Snow Queen.' She looked down at her little sister, who had been edging closer to me and now stood with her forehead resting against Megan's arm.

'Thank you. You are a good teacher.' I glanced at the youngest of the sisters and tried to imagine the world as she saw it. I created a snow scene in my head, a queen dressed in white. I felt moisture building in my eyes, so took a deep breath and busied myself with my sampler.

'What's that?'

'It's a kind of atmospheric sampler,' I told her. 'I'm collecting samples of air. It's for work. Boring.'

'Samples of what? What's in the air?'

'Oh, it takes a reading for humidity, particulate concentration....' I said dismissively. *And records all the words of our conversation,* I wanted to tell her, *to see how they fit into similar patterns in the next biotic community we sample.* But longing for the Snow Queen – how will that sit in the framework?

'What particles?' she pressed, as if hoping for secrets.

'Oh, just some boring chemicals and bits of smoke and pollen.' I expected her to lose interest, but her eyes remained fixed on mine. 'Some spores... all normal.' I waited, but she showed no signs of boredom. 'Do you want to see the Snow Queen too?'

She looked down at the ground, then back at me. She grinned timidly. 'I wouldn't mind.'

I reached into the storage slot of my safety suit and pulled out a packet of currency. 'Here,' I offered, 'buy tickets. Tell your father I won the numbers game,' I put the paper into her hands. I left the cubicle before she could say anything. Numb and sweaty, I didn't trust myself to look back.

138

I found Pedra next to the sheep pens, already calibrating her sampler – she is such a fast worker – and ignoring the guidebook rules as usual. Strange specimens surrounded her, dressed in thick black costumes and carrying helmets. She saw me and broke away from them.

'Did you get what you need?' she asked.

I nodded. 'And a little more. But what have you been doing?'

'I got lots of rare microflora no longer seen – a species of *Pseudomonas* I'm sure they aren't aware of. These are the animals that graze around the limestone wilderness. Ah Calia, their fleeces are so thick – '

'No,' I stopped her firmly. 'I mean with those other specimens.'

'Oh, those are the motorbike riders! I forgot to tell you,' Pedra packed her sampler away. 'There's a PhD student working on the Sunday Motorbiking Phenomenon – they travel for miles and gather in groups around food service outlets. He's among us now somewhere – a boy from Stockholm.'

'What does he look like?' I asked.

'Early twenties in years. Dressed in motor costume.'

'So we will not know him.'

'Only by his sampler.'

'Sounds like an insane waste of time.' My denuder was blocked. That meant all of the emotional residue that should have been trapped on the resin would have either escaped or turned into an un-sortable chemical mass. Somehow, I could not manage to care.

'He's just looking for patterns like the rest of us,' said Pedra. She sighed as we walked away from the auction place. 'I want to go right up into those hills...'

I followed her gaze and breathed deeply. The wind smelt of moorland; moss; peat. I looked at her. 'Perhaps if you followed the guide more carefully …'

We spent the following morning at Sunderland Point. Our line manager wants to look at salt balance in the crabs of this region, so we needed an array of samples.

It was low tide. Both of us were silent on arrival. I had not prepared myself for the shock of seeing an open coast with no army bases, no fences, and from the look on her face, neither had Pedra. 'Look at the grass bending in the wind,' she said. 'And the sky! So white...'

'Right. Lets just think about the order in which we're going to do this, shall we?'

She stared at me for a moment, then began to unpack the equipment.

'Brackish fauna,' I said cheerfully as we set to work. 'I love it.' I always liked to imagine a free sea shore as a mythical place complete with mermaids, and this peninsula almost fulfilled that. The sky was huge, and the sight of birds actually flying freely was still like a dream. Then two motorbikes roared past on the narrow road behind us, breaking the spell. Their helmets glinted like jewels and I stared as they passed, but Pedra did not raise her head.

After a while she said, 'I'm just going to the shore for a moment.'

There was nothing troubling in her voice, so I carried on turning up stones and said, 'I'll carry on here for three more, and then I'll take the high path and get some soil cores. Join me at Sector 2124.'

Time passed. I had my cores and some *Spartina anglica* too, just in case, but there was no sign of Pedra. I walked back along the rough path into the wind. Sometimes you can feel things coming; somehow, I had known Pedra would not arrive, but I was unprepared for the sudden shocking animal noise that ripped through my ears – there was a canine patrolling the top of a garden wall.

I veered off the path and it continued to snarl at me, its warnings urgent and terrifying. I tried to remember what I had learned about such creatures, but my thoughts were mangled by the snap of its teeth with each outburst. I just ran. The sharpness of the noise left a taste in my mouth. I headed for the shore, tripping over myself.

Earlier, on our journey here, we had passed a public vehicle with space for many people and a sign on the front proclaiming *KIRKBY LONSDALE VIA NEWTON*. Of course, Pedra and I had been nervous about the Newton part of the text, but we studied the map and it turned out to be a harmless hamlet. Or so we thought. But now this guard animal perched at head height, just like the wolf chimera in Newton before the sociologists were stopped, before the explosions began. A shiver took over my spine and my thoughts returned to Pedra. Where was she?

Then I saw her on the windswept mud flats, no longer alone. She stood with the motorbike riders that had passed us earlier, and I recalled the specimens she had befriended at the auction. They were surely not the same riders? Their words intertwined with bird calls far above: the song of the sea.

'Pedra!' I crossed the rough ground as fast as I dared while Pedra walked towards me slowly, her steps composed and deliberate. When we met I could see it in her face: she was staying with them. I shook my head at her.

'He'll take me to a place so high that you can hear a bird's wing bend the air. A wild, beautiful place. I'm going to learn so much, Calia.'

'This,' I gestured towards the specimens, 'is not learning!'

'I will be studying their lives.'

'Studying? On your own? Without permission? That is not studying, Pedra. That is recklessness. Suicide. With these... these motor-riders!'

'They are called Bikers, Calia. And the life of a Biker is one of freedom and deep thought.'

'I could report you.'

'Don't. Please.'

I stared at her, speechless.

'I'll be somewhere so remote they'll never find me.'

'You will not survive.'

'They will look after me. They are related to an ancient branch of Bikers called the Satan's Slaves. They are special.'

I shook my head again. I looked over her shoulder at the riders. Thin sunlight bathed the scene. Their murmurings were

141

companionable, like the rhythmic munching of sheep, and contributed to a vision of peace and contentment the like of which I had rarely experienced.

~

It has been over fifteen hours since I saw Pedra. The Cottage is on a sloping road and overlooks a meadow that dips down to the stream that I have been staring at for much of that time. It runs like a silver thread in this half-light. I have not settled into a healthy sleeping pattern since we set up camp here – it is hard to sleep on such a *solid* surface – but since hearing from our line manager last night that the Scandinavian boy has also broken free, thoughts of Pedra and her fate have not left my mind. Sleep is far beyond me now, and look – the dawn is here. It is pink and delicate: the insomniac's reward.

I hear the clip-clomping of hooves before I see them, like something blowing towards me on the wind. A dream of a scene. I shake my head to be sure I am really seeing it: a herd of cows walks down the middle of the road. Walking through the village, led at one end by an ancient farmer, and at their rear, yes! There he is: the young, round-faced son with the many words. *Saves getting them into trailers. It's only twice a year.*

Huge swaying bodies, graceful in their way. A smidgeon of worry in their eyes; perhaps they want to get where they are going. I think of the two farmer's daughters. *Going out of milk.* I think of Pedra far away in her hills. We were to travel to the Great Stone of Fourstones today. That would have suited Pedra. She is determined to see one of the last curlews.

The herd disappears and a breeze sets the ivy rustling and rubbing against the window. I may not continue here without her.

Skylarks over Ingleborough
Mary Sylvia Winter

They mate, hatch, grow, rest, sleep on the ground.

Yet to us they are skyborne,
only seeming real when that tangled thread of sound
tugs our eyes upwards.
So here we stand
motionless in mid-climb
   necks cricked and eyes sun-scorched
searching for that one – there! that one –
the spinner of that drifting thread
before it drops again and is silent.

Once they are down, we never look for their nests.
We'd never find them, we assure each other.
Or at least not without stepping on eggs first.
Or is the truth that,
once their flying song has ceased,
we no longer believe in them?
And why should we?
There is always another skylark to search for, and another,
so that we keep on thinking of them as skyborne,
even though they mate, hatch, grow, rest and sleep on the ground.

After a while we plod on.
Plodding is what we do now for most of our time together.
Flight comes seldom, and never lasted long anyway.
These other climbing couples,
are they perhaps the same?
They look ground-based;
overheard snatches speak of insurance policies,
    children's school reports,
        bathroom tiles,
            and how fed up she is of the way he reads the paper
                when she's trying to talk to him.
Yet always, somewhere
there is a note of ecstasy to be heard
from a few who are definitely soaring –
maybe even, now and then,
    still
        from us.
And so we go on thinking of love as skyborne,
even though plodding is what we do now
    for most of our time together.

Elemental
Clare Weze Easterby

Luis Holland stands on an empty field watching as the last remnants of Wray Fair are dismantled. Vans churn up the turf and bouncy castles deflate sadly. I turned up for the interview expecting a devastating Inspector Felling smile, along with an arch from that famous eyebrow, but recent events have left Holland time for none of that. He's here to open the Scarecrow Festival, an annual event that attracts thousands of visitors to this small Lancashire village. 'I've been coming here with my nephews for the last couple of years and that's why I agreed to open for them,' he says, 'but I never dreamed I'd be telling the world about something like this.'

He's in good company. When this paper booked our interview, I couldn't have predicted that the man who has played Felling since 2005 would be an eyewitness to one of the most surreal events of the decade. I ask him if last night's atmosphere – the late hour, the drum parade, the lanterns, the dancing figures, the elements of the rites of spring – might have played tricks on the collective imagination.

'No,' he says. 'There were definitely other figures dancing with them. Those scarecrows may be tall, but some of them were doing things that aren't humanly possible. And the Winter scarecrow still hasn't been found.'

The irony is not lost on Holland. 'I've spent much of my recent working life pretending to chase and understand the supernatural,' he says. 'And now this. People will be cynical, but it's pure coincidence.' He found himself standing next to 'a random cameraman' and together they created an on-the-scene report, complete with commentary from Holland. 'I knew it would make the morning papers and the news, but I didn't have much choice. I was there and it was happening.'

Holland might plead amazement, but this episode sits well with his luck-laden and unconventional life so far. Despite his youth, this is a man whose theatrical prowess is legendary. His well judged Dr Faustus in 2002 took him from relative obscurity to his TV breakthrough in *Felling*, the urbane detective solving ghost mysteries at the turn of the last century.

When I ask him about last night's occurrence, which, quite frankly, takes some believing, he's adamant that there's no exaggeration in any of the news bulletins. 'It was palpable. People were absolutely awestruck. There's a little cottage on the side of the road just next to place where the first of the huge scarecrows went down. The people standing in the doorway of that cottage must have had the fright of their lives.'

So what did he think came out of the shadows last night?

'Something primal. Something harking back to … I don't know...'

Bacchus? In Britain?

He looks at me as if I'm demented. 'No, the one I saw was much less bulbous and jovial than that. Pretty grotesque in appearance, actually, close up. Folds of loose skin under its neck. Eyes like jelly.'

We cross the field, walk through the churchyard and emerge in Main Street. Not just somebody dressed up and walking on stilts, then?

'Definitely not. The face was real and its expression changed. It wasn't some blank-faced scarecrow.'

Holland is a Londoner by birth and still keeps a home there. This village feels a million miles from the congested roads and pollution of the capital. Perhaps when visitors descend in spring they are overwhelmed by the sheer bucolic verdancy of such a spacious, natural environment. As we stand in front of the church gates, where a crow-shaped scarecrow leers at us, I put it to him that perhaps he was infected by this same green fever, but he shakes his head. 'The sheer size and power of it was unmistakable,' he says.

The cameraman must have been doing his pieces, I say, trying to get the full height and girth of this thing in view if it moved so fast. 'It was quite dangerous for him actually,' he says, and goes on to describe the chasing and tripping, launching into one of his famous lunges and pointing to the spot on School Lane where the entity allegedly drew itself up to its full height and gyrated before climbing the gable end and disappearing over the rooftop with superhuman speed.

Where did it go next? 'Nobody has any idea, but I would have said it carried on in that direction,' he points over the rooftops, 'there are woods upriver. It's wild and beautiful.' He lifts his hands in the classic 'these are the facts we have to hand' gesture which features somewhere in a *Felling* scene each week.

Barkin Bridge is somewhere up that way, I offer, and so is Drunken Bridge. He laughs politely, but doesn't take the bait.

He is diffident over some of the details reported in the media. The entity was said to have rattled a stuffed animal in the face of one of the festival organisers in an 'I told you so' manner. 'I didn't see that,' says Holland. 'In fact, the stuffed animal changes according to who you speak to. I've heard it was a hedgehog, a cat, and even a badger. I think you can take those tales with a heavy dose of salt...' He trails off as someone comes up to us and asks for his autograph.

I tell him that all the eyewitnesses I've asked are also adamant that other figures were dancing with the tallest

151

scarecrows from the start of the rites of spring ceremony. A child told me that 'The one with the icy moustache' was quite plainly pulling the autumn figure towards the river, and that whoever was operating Autumn didn't want to go. They were fighting.

Holland looks intrigued. 'I didn't see the very beginning,' he admits, 'but I heard it involved a skirmish outside the Tea Rooms. When I went past earlier, they were still clearing up the wood shavings.'

Whatever the outcome of the investigation into last night's events, *Felling* looks set to run and run, and it's safe to assume that the Wray Fair Incident will only bolster Luis Holland's reign over stage and screen and keep those Baftas flowing.

A Short Time Ago on Newby Moor
Clare Weze Easterby

The postman was the first to bring the news, but nobody believed him.

'They're going to build a hotel on Newby Moor.'

'On *Newby Moor*?'

Then the rumour changed – it wasn't a hotel, it was a delicatessen. Then a restaurant.

Who was behind it?

Nobody knew.

There was no way that plans would be passed for a building on Newby Moor of all places…

But passed they were. The structure went up and began to take shape and soon there was a small mansion in the middle of the moor, looking like it had been there for centuries. You can use aged, reclaimed stone these days, we said, but what about the landscaping?

'Nothing will grow in that wind. It'll look a right bare

155

beggar.'

But windbreaks and follies were built with planting behind them, so shrubs were sheltered.

They hadn't refurbished an existing building in one of the villages – that was what nobody could understand. *Another white elephant. It'll never take off in this credit-crunched climate…* and people waited, sagely, to see how long the mad venture would last. There were too many things going on under the one roof: café and restaurant and bar and boutique and gift shop and country house hotel all rolled into one. Everything-cum-nothing. And you had to drive to it, which was completely wrong. It should have been in a village.

A group of friends from Bentham were the first to investigate.

'Everything seems to be called a salon, somehow. There's a salon for sipping coffee, a salon full of clothes, a salon for viewing paintings and an Internet salon, but no hairdresser's. I can't understand it.'

'Nice coffee, though.'

'Yes and I saw a lovely pair of shoes in the boutique; I might go back and treat myself to those. But I still can't see it paying for itself in the long run.'

'I'll tell you what – I had a mushroom soup in that cafe that tasted like nothing on this Earth.'

'The play area's got real toys instead of soft play. There's dolls houses, car tracks, little art and modelling tables – it's just lovely.'

'Yes, and there's chess and table tennis for the older ones instead of computer games.'

'Good God, it was a piece of heaven, that soup. Makes everything else I've had seem like wallpaper paste.'

Three playgroups got together and funded a children's party in the 'parent's salon'. The children loved the mini-maze and ran round it all afternoon, shrieking. The garden, everyone agreed, was strangely warm, strangely sheltered. 'It shouldn't be – it should be blowing like a good 'un, even behind these walls.' It was peculiar – everyone said so – but they'd all loved watching

156

the children play.

News of their findings spread to Burton in Lonsdale, where The Newby Moor Emporium was chosen as the venue for the Mummers planning meeting.

'Who's t'owner then?'

'You never see him. Keeps in t'background, never talks to people.'

'Nobody wants to be hostile to offcomed-uns, but this gent just popped up from nowhere – the first anyone heard of him was when he paced the site out with the architect.'

Word also filtered around the villages that it was possible to while away whole afternoons or evenings on those squashy leather sofas and nobody expected you to buy more than a cursory coffee or two. And if the owner did appear – a fleeting figure in doorways and back rooms here and there that no-one seemed to get a good look at – there was an indulgent, Father Christmas-like aura about him.

A lot of dressing up went on in the boutique. There was a small catwalk, music to play as friends sashayed down it, yet more comfy seating in velvet and leather and sales assistants who encouraged little shows: they usually increased sales. If an expensive item was modelled, it made the cheaper versions on the rails look very attractive. The atmosphere of opulence seemed almost too good to be true.

'When something looks too good to be true, it usually is,' said somebody's husband, but he said it without much conviction, smothered inside a joke.

'I tried on this dress. Well. It was nothing like you've ever seen in your life before. I couldn't believe it.'

'One room smells like you're in a pine forest.'

'I like the second floor best. The mezzanines and skylights.'

'Something for everyone.'

~

That was what attracted the local press: *there's something for everyone*. The statement was repeated by the first customer Nick interviewed. 'And one room just seems to flow into the next.' The lady was glassy-eyed and spoke slowly. Nick looked around the coffee salon and nobody was doing much talking. It was the same in the bar. Still, quiet people, content, like sheep, grazing on nuts and sipping drinks, and it was only five-fifteen. That was worth noting.

It was one of his first assignments, so he hadn't completely got to grips with the *Who, What, Where, When* and *Why* of things, but next, he scrutinised the place itself. Yes, it was all beautifully finished, yes, all the materials were organic, but they were *too* organic. Cotton and sheepskin and wood and wool are comforting, but altogether, the place was chilling. Everything brand new yet looking as though it had been there forever. The white stone reminded him of bone. He couldn't shake the knowledge that the sheepskin and suede were actually skin and hair, and they felt wrong, like ivory and leopard skin. That was worth noting too.

He went to the counter and ordered an orange juice. 'Is the boss available?'

The girl serving him didn't look as if she could be bothered to talk. She had a round face and very shiny brown hair that she smoothed behind her ears at regular intervals. 'Don't know if he's back.' She called out to a slim girl on her way to the sink,' Boss about?'

'I haven't seen him since this morning.' The girl at the sink smiled at Nick, then started to stack dishes.

The barmaid intervened. 'Glass collection first, Isla.' A look passed between them.

Staff are great, his manager had told him. Staff in shops, staff in bars, they've all got their favourite way of remembering buying patterns, and "their own antenna for spotting the unusual. Use them". This girl didn't look like she could spot the froth on a beer.

'Good to work for is he? Where's he from?'

The girl shrugged. Nick tried a wider smile; his baby face sometimes eased his path. 'Well, where does he sound like he's from?'

The barmaid looked him in the eye then passed her glance

over as much of him as she could see over the bar. She shrugged. 'Nowhere. You can't tell.'

Nick took the orange juice to a table, where he made a surreptitious note of this too. *No discernible accent.*

Passing from room to room, Nick took in the smell of supper and the feeling of fellowship and holidays in the restaurant, the wafting coffee smells in the mezzanine salons. He sucked it all up, watching everything as if it were a film.

The gardens were on three levels with the roof terrace leading off from one of the boutiques. Nick climbed the old stone steps, enjoying the pull on his legs, then almost collided with a small boy haring down them, wielding some kind of superhero's vehicle, which caught his sleeve. He sat on a bench in front of a water feature spurting from a carpet of gypsophila and went over his notes. After a moment, the slim girl from the bar came out of a side door and leaned against the wall behind him with a steaming cup. Isla. She looked worried. Or sad. Perhaps both.

Nick got to his feet and tried to look as if he'd been ready for a spot of wall leaning all along. *Who, What, Where, When* and *Why* he thought, and plunged in. 'Hello again. Everything all right?'

The girl looked at him. 'Oh, hi,' she said, and was her face hopeful? Pleased? A bit shy? 'Yes, fine. Are you lost?'

'No, just taking it all in.'

'Well, there's plenty to do here.'

'Not that you get much time I bet.'

She smiled. 'It's my first week. I haven't got the hang of things yet.'

Nick pulled at his earlobe and thought. 'Sent you for sky-hooks, have they?' It came out with just the right blend of empathy and humour and she smiled again. He felt emboldened, easier. The wall felt gritty on his back but he didn't want to alter this perfect position. They both looked out at the blue-grey moor beyond the terrace. It was like a scene from a summer storm. Cloud shadows sculled over the land. A bird with a soulful, wheedling cry swooped somewhere above their heads. And then he asked the question that broke the dream. 'Do you live on the

159

job?'

'No. I live with my boyfriend.'

Neither spoke. Nick concentrated harder on the moor, on Ingleborough, purple in the distance. 'How do you get on with the boss?' he asked after a while.

She studied the climbing roses that tumbled over the trellis-work beside her. 'We don't really see that much of him.'

'It's a strange place to choose for a business like this though, isn't it? Rumour has it that he drugged the planning authorities.'

She giggled.

'Tried to get an appointment with him before I came. I'm here for the *Tribune*, everyone's intrigued about this place. But he never returns any calls.'

'Ooh – are you a food critic?'

'No, I'm just a trainee.' Nick stepped away from the wall and looked around the terrace. 'He's everywhere I look, but he's nowhere.'

Isla looked at him as if he'd revealed a great truth and he racked his brains for the right thing to say, but then a voice called through from inside the building, from a room that seemed to be a mirror image of one he'd been in earlier. 'Isla! Can you push through that veg prep now please? You've had twenty-five minutes. Did you realise that?'

He stared through the door after Isla had gone, marvelling at the trick of perspective. Would Isla know something, if there was anything to know? The thought expanded inside him like a drug and he felt spooked and excited; things might yet get more intriguing. He left the public face of the building and explored round the back, where the weather made an appearance for the first time. The wind felt like it came straight from Ingleborough. He paused at the top of another set of stone steps leading all the way down to ground level and wrote in his notebook:

<u>Where</u>: the moor-building interface.

The steps led to a wasteland where rows of shrubs waited in pots amid odd slates and piles of stones. At the far end of the space, where the moor hadn't yet been pushed back completely,

160

Nick found a door marked 'Private'. The owner's office? He walked up to it and knocked, then waited, preparing his lines. Nothing moved. He tried the door and it opened. Better and better! Should he just go inside? He looked over his shoulder and around. The shrubs shivered in the wind, like dozens of miniature people nodding *Yes*.

'Hello?' he called. He peered through the window; the room was unoccupied and unlit. There were rules about this sort of thing... *sod it*. He went inside and pulled the door closed behind him.

Inside, the possibilities were endless, but the sound of his heartbeat loud in his ear made concentration difficult. The room was low-ceilinged and smelt of damp plaster, warm plastic, computers and freshly opened paper reams. It was half finished – the floor was still concrete, the three desks arranged haphazardly, only one chair, no visible telephones. He walked over to the smallest desk, attracted by a used coffee cup. Next to it were two stacks of A4 pages full of names printed in an unusual font he couldn't name. Staff? No, too many. Customer database?

He moved on to the back of the room and there was the server, humming gently. Quite ordinary. Except that he had the feeling there was a different kind of engine inside it, something that was working very hard to keep the whole place going, pumping, like a heart.

The sight of his own legs walking through the room, his own arms and hands poking around surprised him, in a light-headed, *deja vu* kind of way, as if he hadn't eaten anything for hours. He bent close to the server and breathed in the smell of warm electric circuits. It was almost six pm, but it felt like more than just one day was ending. He let out a laughing sigh – he could have sworn he was braver than this. He took out his notebook and scribbled down a room description, angling the pad towards the daylight. Fast, he thought, or there won't be time to find out if there's anything to find out. *Names*, he wrote. *People collection. Why?*

There was a noise outside near the door and he stopped moving. The noise wasn't repeated, but perhaps somebody had locked the room. He stood still in the silence. Stupid, *stupid* idiot. And this was only week four. Heat rose in him and a flood of scenes marched through his head; the new landlord explaining unfathomable things about the boiler; Mum telling him off about leaving clothes piled up in corners; the embarrassing escorted tour on his first day at work; Emily last year when she wouldn't be told it was over; the headteacher in the sixth form when he'd been caught smoking. He wanted to crouch, to bask in the cool air closer to the ground, but it would be cold later if he really was locked in here.

He darted for the door. Adrenaline surged, his fingertips throbbed with it, but he managed to turn the handle – and it opened. He stepped outside, smiling in the light, sniffing in the smell of moss from the moor then laughed – he'd had his mobile in his pocket anyway, so why all the sweat? Ridiculous.

Then a figure appeared above him, seemingly from nowhere... a large shape outlined against the cloudy sky.

It had to be the proprietor. He loomed over the top of the steps like a pirate ship, loose jacket flapping, lengthy grey hair blowing straight up from his head like a halo. By the time he reached the bottom, Nick's brain had retrieved and processed a dozen instructions from the boss on how to handle these encounters, but his madly, almost painfully thumping heart got in the way of any sense. He could scarcely hear anything.

'How can I help *you*?' The man had a close cut, grey beard, a sharp nose and highly shined shoes. He wasn't young, but his build was solid and powerful, his hair thick and smooth now that the wind had dropped it.

Nick held out his hand, feeling thin and weedy. 'Nick Mason – *The Tribune*. My office has been trying to get hold of you for a while.' He swallowed. The man didn't take his hand for a long, heat-flooded moment, and he felt so weak he wanted to sit down.

The proprietor grinned. 'We're not at the interview stage just yet.' He stared at Nick and dropped his hand after a quick, sharp shake. 'We want to find our feet before we get pigeonholed in any way.'

162

The eye contact continued until Nick broke it. He curled his hand around his notebook in his pocket. He knows I've been inside, he thought. 'We?'

'We're a consortium.' The word was presented like a deal-sealing ID card. As the barmaid had said, the voice wasn't northern, nor obviously southern; Nick could only think what it wasn't. Now the man was silent, his thin lips unsmiling.

'Well, when you're ready we'd be grateful if you could get in touch. We'd like to do a feature,' Nick's voice sounded fragile, stunted. 'This project is so different from anything that's gone before, and our readers would be fascinated to find out what... find out about the thinking behind it.'

The proprietor folded his arms, still staring. 'This is just the beginning.' Smoothly, he began to walk Nick back up the steps and into the people, the coffee, the clothes and the waving gypsophila. This was the future, he said, together with wind farms and polytunnels, proper management of the Waterfalls, and even Ingleborough itself. It was spiel and Nick could lock onto none of it. He thought of the list of names on that desk. A collection of people. A pied piper.

They reached the boutique terrace, where Isla stood with a tall, skinny man in baggy trousers with close-cropped dark hair and bored eyes; the boyfriend. They were going inside. The boyfriend went first, going through the door without really holding or passing it to her, like a child might, and Isla paused to smile as Nick and the proprietor went by.

'Nice to have met you Mr Mason. We'll be in touch.' The proprietor didn't hold out his hand for a shake. Neither did he invite him back into the building, so there was nothing else for Nick to do but walk away. After two steps he turned round to see Isla still gazing after him, as if he were a dream or a ghost. The proprietor disappeared into his emporium. Nick waved. She waved back and smiled, her face full of wishes.

~

Go to the emporium next time you're passing over Newby Moor. Throw yourself down in one of his squashy chairs. Have a

163

frothy coffee. The lights will glow and dim to suit the time of day. All your worries will vanish with a mouthful of cupcake, you'll hear only the soothing swish of the wind rippling over the moor – and there's something for everyone.

Cloud over Roeburndale
--for Sheila
Mary Sylvia Winter

Driving up the Moor,
between hiss of wind and clatter of beck
I see above your farm
the shadow-rippled acreage
sun-sporting summits
of the clouds.

Their kingdom has its own laws.
They can with impunity
    flood your valley
    break bridges
    sepulchre sheep in snow
    drench hour-old lambs
    and feed them to the crows.

Yet now, mounting higher,
it seems to me that their lambent immensity
might soften, a little,
even grief,
loneliness,
    the endless round of toil.

Or perhaps it is simply
that here above the cosy clutter of trees
there is nothing to stop our seeing
that the sky beyond the clouds is endless
    and incandescent with light.

Grandmother's Footsteps
Clare Weze Easterby

We were playing castles in a ruin near Ingleton Waterfalls walk. Four of us had sneaked out. It was one of those times when each set of parents thinks the others are minding the kids. I love those times, and with three families on holiday together in a house like

169

a mansion, we had loads of chances to get away.

'Lets go up to that bit where the path goes through the farm,' said Sol.

'That's miles!' said Emma, but we all trundled off behind Sol and eventually, without anyone really noticing, we'd left the path altogether.

'Hey, we're as high as the clouds!' said Jake. 'We're mountaineering!' and we were. The Waterfalls gorge looked like another country, far away below us in miniature.

Then we saw the boy.

It was weird, because he appeared in front of us so suddenly, a big, muscly boy with no neck and one of those mouths that always looks too wet. Stupid brown trousers, like his mum had made him wear them for playing out.

'You won't get back to the path that way,' he said.

As if we'd asked him anyway, I thought, *Where did you spring from?*

'You shouldn't try to do the Waterfalls walk backwards,' he said. 'It gets my goat when people do that.'

What goat? I thought. 'Who said we were?' I said. We'd done the walk the day before—Tom and Sol and their mum and dad, Oliver and Emma and theirs, and me and Jake and ours—all three families together. 'Anyway, *you're* not on the path!'

The boy said, 'I can understand why you'd want to get up into the fresh air, but really, you're trespassing.'

I looked at the others but none of them said anything. 'Are you from the farm?' I asked. He didn't look like a farm boy—in fact, he didn't look like anything I'd ever seen—but why else would he be there like some kind of guard?

'People are always getting lost round here,' he said, as if I hadn't asked a question. 'Come on, I'll take you down.'

He set off down the hill without looking back at us, and a bunch of midges that had been circling the air just above his head set off too.

'Come on,' said Sol, following.

I held my hands up. 'No! What're you doing?'

'We might as well.' Sol shrugged and the others went with

170

him. I hesitated for a second, then joined them. It was the summer holidays, but it hadn't been really sunny yet and didn't look as if it ever would be. The lower we went the more flies we collected and the crosser I got.

And then it was somehow as if he thought he'd known us for ages. He started a game of tig which we're all miles too old for, but for some mad reason, the others all joined in.

'Hey look,' he said when the game had calmed down and everyone was standing panting. 'Look what I found.' He reached into a pocket and pulled out a handful of coloured stones. 'Enough for one each.'

Everyone took one. Everyone except me.

'What's up, Liam?' murmured Jake.

I couldn't tell him. I didn't want to take anything from the strange boy. Not only did I not want to keep anything he'd give me, but I didn't even want to touch anything he'd touched. 'What's your name anyway?' I said, as if I was accusing him of a crime.

'Tight,' said Sol. I glared at him.

'Bart,' said the boy.

Sol made a face at me and I shook my head. I wanted to remind him of yesterday, when I'd saved him from getting into trouble over completely snapping my mum's necklace. Most of all I wanted to tell everyone a joke about the mansion, something this stranger wouldn't get, just so we could all laugh except him.

'Hey.' I fake-chuckled. 'D'you know why our dad made sure we visited Wigglesworth and Giggleswick first?' They shook their heads. I paused dramatically. 'Because their names are really "out there." My dad said those actual words! He said "out there!"'

'That's soft, man,' said Sol, but then his mum's so cool she even knows who Eminem is.

Bart set off walking again. 'All this was under the sea once,' he said to the air. Just like last time, he didn't bother looking to see if we followed, and just like last time, we all did. 'It was warm. Not that deep. There were coral reefs.'

We all looked at each other.

'Different creatures evolved when the land was reclaimed by the sea. Creatures were trapped in pockets. Creatures like you

171

wouldn't believe.'

Emma's eyes went round. We all looked at each other again.

At last! I thought. 'That couldn't happen.'

'Frozen when the Ice Age came, they were locked in suspended animation, waiting for it to get warm enough for them to come alive again.'

We'd come to a shed in the middle of nowhere. Not a barn, a shed. It looked spooky.

'Hey look at this!' said Emma, pointing to a wasp-trap jar. 'Who's left this when there's nobody here?'

Bart didn't look curious at all. He carried on walking.

'Honestly!' I hissed. 'We shouldn't be following him!'

Nobody disagreed with me, but still everyone followed.

Bart looked at the sky. 'It's going to rain. At least we're not on Titan. It rains methane there. Stinky fart rain.' He turned to me and licked his fat, red, wet lips. 'Titan is one of Saturn's moons,' he added, as if I could never have known such a thing in a million years.

'So what?' I said. 'We can all use Google, you know.'

He made his hands into binoculars and scanned the horizon. 'Right,' he said. 'I know this way looks the easiest, but the best way is actually up over towards Ingleborough and through that clump of trees.'

We had come to a fork in the path. We could see a half-familiar field down a clear, grassy path, while the other way led into a dark, wooded area. Tom looked like he'd read my mind and was looking longingly in the easy direction.

'We know the way back now,' I said, looking at each of the others in turn. 'Come on.' I herded them down onto the nice, safe, clear path, ignoring Bart and his ridiculous woods idea.

'That's really not a good way!' croaked Bart. We all turned to look at his face: he was frightened. He looked cold too, all of a sudden; he hugged his arms around himself like it was winter.

Emma looked like she might start crying.

It's weird but I can't remember us saying 'Goodbye' or 'See you, loser' or anything. I just remember that we were on our own again, and going in *my* direction, away from those trees, away

172

from that boy. Everyone now had their own little band of midges hovering around their hair, moving in time as we moved, like living shadows.

We walked and walked and Bart was right about one thing: it started raining. There was no shelter, nothing to do except plough on through it. We were dripping, trainers squelchy, noses like mini-waterfalls. I don't think I've ever been so sopping.

'Short cut,' said Sol. 'Through this field.'

We climbed a gate.

'It's massive!' said Tom.

It was. It rose in the middle and a ridge dropped off over the horizon, so we couldn't see what was on the other side. The rain slowed down to a drizzle.

'This is better,' said Sol. 'Shouldn't be long now.'

But it was a cow field. We didn't find that out until we were halfway through it, and when the cows saw us, they came towards us. Slowly at first, then faster. Then galloping. We ran, but the faster we ran, the faster they ran.

They might not be able to stop, I thought. *That's the thing.* 'Stop!' I shouted. 'We're going to get trampled!'

I turned around and took one step towards the cows. The others stopped too. So did the cows. I don't know how I knew what to do. I'm not used to cows. They stood and stared at us, so we set off again, in a more controlled way this time. But as soon as our backs were turned, the cows did the same. We stopped, turned and faced them again.

'They've stopped,' said Tom. 'It's like Grandmother's footsteps.'

'Walk backwards,' said Jake. 'They can't do it if you're looking at them. It's like Doctor Who.'

And that kind of worked, in a scary sort of way. One moment we seemed to have got a fair distance away, the next, they were almost on top of us, breathing hard, with long threads of mucous dangling from their mouths and noses. And staring— always staring.

'They're looking at me funny,' said Emma.

'They're looking at all of us,' I said.

173

It took a long, long time, but eventually we reached the gate at the other end of the field. We could see the path from there. Legs bashed legs as we all scrambled over the gate at the same time. And once we were safely on the other side, I could feel how shaky my breath was and how hard my heart was beating.

'Should have gone Bart's way,' said Emma.

The Shepherd
for J.G.
Mary Sylvia Winter

City-bred, I cultivate my new farming neighbours
      with naïve enthusiasm.
If a gate needs opening, I open it –
      and shut it, of *course.*
That is how we find ourselves
in this muddy field in April,
I in wellies and my son in his pushchair.
Curious, I have followed the tractor in
      (having courteously opened – and shut – the gate)
      and am awaiting developments.

The young farmer waves his thanks,
then climbs down and opens the door of a small trailer.
Six or seven ewes scuttle out,
      half tripping over a milling crowd of lambs
      --their own, presumably.
The spring air is filled with their cries
      of overdone anxiety.
The farmer walks among them, dealing out lambs
      --one over here, two over there.
I am puzzled; do these ewes not know their own lambs?
"T'trip down'll 'ave confused 'e,", he explains.
      "Could tek 'em awhile to sort th'selves out."
I am still puzzled. Does he mean to tell me he knows
      which lambs go with which ewes?
"Oh aye. Pretty much."
Nothing special. All in a day's work.

He carries on, and I am left staring.
Of course we all know where those lambs are headed
eventually,
But just for now,
        in this field in April,
        today and in Lancashire,
the shepherd who knows his sheep
is made flesh and dwells among us.

The Sun God of Lancashire
Mary Sylvia Winter

It's easy to believe in a sun god
if you live in Lancashire
--not because he's there all the time,
but because of the way he isn't.
We survive floods, dreadful harvests and months
of short days
only through faith that he will one day return.
And whenever a stray sunbeam touches our faces
our hearts leap and thrill.
Surely only a god
could inspire such gratitude.
We know that without him we are nothing
--that's obvious enough.
He draws us to himself;
we flock after him to Spain, to Tenerife
--places where he smiles all the time.
He must like the people there better.
Here he wraps himself in rain,
and our clouds hide his face from us.
Turn again to us, and we shall be whole.
We curse the rain
    --but nobody ever curses the sun.

In memory of Agnes and William Bradley
of Selber Farm, Westhouse